SOME SORT OF BEAUTY

First published in 2012
by Bradshaw Books
Tigh Filí, Civic Trust House, 50 Pope's Quay, Cork
www.bradshawbooks.com

ISBN: 978 1 905374 29 8

Cover Photograph: Stephanie Höpner / Source: PHOTOCASE
Author Headshot (Page 138): Andy Ferreira (www.andyferreira.com)

10 9 8 7 6 5 4 3 2 1

 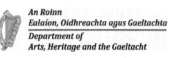

An Roinn
Ealaíon, Oidhreachta agus Gaeltachta
Department of
Arts, Heritage and the Gaeltacht

SOME SORT OF BEAUTY
Stories

Jamie O'Connell

bradshaw books

For my grandfather
Tom O'Connell

'Go into yourself. Search for the reason that bids you to write… describe your sorrows and desires, passing thoughts and a belief in some sort of beauty'

Rainer Maria Rilke, *Letters to a Young Poet: Letter One*

Contents

Without Art

I'll be sitting outside the café where we used to have afternoon coffees and fight over who'd read *The Sunday Times Style* magazine first. The table will wobble because of the uneven gravel, adding a certain apprehension as I put my cup down after each sip. I'll remember the past, wondering if you'll be different. You didn't sound different on the phone. Granted, it was an awkward sort of a chat.

It'll be a Sunday afternoon in late spring that we'll meet. I'll be dressed in something I think you'll find attractive but won't give the impression that I've tried too hard. I'll straighten my white T-shirt; it'll be less brazen than the wife-beaters I wore when I was nineteen and I was trying to catch your attention. But I was never subtle with my likes; I was always eager (I think you might've said heedless), living with the assumption that no matter how far I took things, the consequences could always be fixed.

I'll sit near the French windows with a full-fat latte (being in my late twenties with grey hairs on my temples, I've long since given up the illusion that if I simply eat protein, fruit and vegetables, wear sunscreen and exercise, I might stay young forever). I'll take a sip, looking out over the fields in front of Fota House, feeling sad as I see the glint of metal bonnets in a distant car park, a reminder that it's not the nineteenth century, despite the fine china, the neo-classical façade of the house and the mature gardens that surround me.

Glancing at my watch, I'll wonder are you going to show up, despite the text saying you're on your way. I'll flick through my old messages, the ones Jen sent me, wishing me well, telling me to ring her after our coffees are over. The possibilities of whether or not you and I could be together again will have been discussed.

You'll walk up the main driveway; I'll notice your blond hair is cut short. I never liked long hair on men, though with you it always had a Kurt Cobainish quality. You'll be wearing Converse, as you always did, your blue eyes and square stubbly chin giving you the look of a teddy bear. I'll move in my seat, questioning if I should stand and give you a hug or if it'll be too awkward. In the end, I'll stay seated.

'Hi Seb,' you'll say. 'Sorry for being late – the parking.'

'You're grand, you're grand. How are you?'

'I'm good. I'll run and get a coffee. D'you want anything?'

'No, no. I'm grand, thanks.'

You'll vanish inside. I'll not look over my shoulder; instead I'll think about each element of your appearance. I'll evaluate how I've aged compared to you, resigned to the fact that I've more greys than you do, despite your being seven years my senior.

I don't know if I'll feel emotional or if the sensation will be more like breathlessness. It won't be like before. I didn't cry at Granddad's funeral, well not at the ceremony anyhow. A silent strength has entered me, something new, like a kind of oil that has permeated who I am.

You'll come back with a latte and a slice of chocolate cake, moaning about the stupid old lady in front of you who deliberated for five minutes over the different scones. You'll be using your 'let's keep things light' tone; you never liked serious chats, making all complaints humorous like a stand-up comedian. I'll laugh, though this will sadden me. I'll worry that our meeting will be a waste of time because we won't talk in any real way.

You'll put two sachets of sugar into your latte. You always had a sweet tooth. I could never persuade you to drink my apple, carrot and celery smoothies, nor could I stop you crash-dieting; your 'only cornflakes for a week' diet never worked, nor did your yoga fascination that rarely went beyond two classes. I'll smile, thinking back on how you were when we were alone. I'll remember that you could even be a bit camp when you wanted, though most people never suspected you were gay until you told them. I, on the other hand, loved pop music and Prada. I was more immediately identifiable. It was often in the subtle things that I felt more masculine, how I hated to be the 'spoonee' when we slept; always the 'spooner', even if you'd just fucked me.

I'll try not to think about sex as you mess with your hair, making it scruffier. In the three years we were together, I don't think I ever stayed over and we didn't fuck. I'd read somewhere that if you put a penny in a jar every time you had sex for the first year and then took one out each time after, you'd never empty the jar. But we emptied it. We even fucked on that final day.

Something was different that morning. The fear was gone. I kissed you and, as you kissed me back, I wondered did you still hope or were you trying to savour the end of our intimacy. I could feel the heat of your thighs. My feet were cold. You pulled the blankets up over our shoulders; I moved on top of you, grabbing your hair as you began thrusting. It wasn't the time to impress, to fuck in ten different ways. It was a full stop, not a flourish. You continued, finally squeezing me tight and I enjoyed the pleasure and the grief of it.

I lay my head on your chest, the room growing cool. The grey morning grew lighter and I could hear the birds outside your window. Then your phone vibrated and you tapped my shoulder and said, 'I don't know, Sebastian. Just decide what you want. Just decide.'

'How's the job?' I'll say. You'll tell me you're working in London for a television company and that you love it, though you hope they'll give you a pay rise as London is stupidly expensive.

'Are you enjoying the PhD? It's the Creative Writing one, right?' you'll ask.

'Yeah, it's great. Plenty of lie-ins,' I'll joke about the little amount of work that I'm doing, selling myself short, as is the typically Irish thing to do. In actual fact, I love the course and the freedom it gives me to read, write and enjoy my solitude. This truth will eventually take over. I'll tell you about my love of the books that I'm reading and my fear that I might never possess the genius of those writers.

'Do you go to Dubai much to see Jen and Paul?' you'll ask about my sister and her husband.

'I "winter" there,' I'll laugh. 'Isn't it great? I get to use "winter" as a verb.'

'You like it there?'

'It's good for holidays and Claire gets bigger every time. But I don't think I could live there. I'm too morose for that amount of sunshine.'

You'll smile.

'Did you go up, what's it called, the tallest building?'

'Yeah, the Burj Khalifa. Paul and I flushed the men's toilets up there a few times – you know its costs two hundred and fifty euros a flush because they have to pump the water all that way up.'

You'll ask me how high it is and I'll exaggerate, telling

you it's the best part of a mile to the top. Hyperbole is the storyteller's tuning fork, allowing words to become narrative in the way sounds become notes; finding the fiction that weaves its way through life. I'll remember the quote, 'without art, the crudeness of reality would make the world unbearable', and think we need these hyperboles so we can love our lives the way we love fiction.

'Will Jen be able to make it back for your book launch?' you'll ask.

'She's coming all right. I've the family under pain of death to attend.'

'What's the collection about?'

'Y'know, I think that's the question writers fear the most. It's named after this German poet who said a writer should look into the ample past of their life for inspiration, to try and find beauty in it.'

I know I sound pretentious when I quote writers whose work is far beyond my own ability. In truth, my love of Rilke's *Letters to a Young Poet* began after I saw an online interview with Lady Gaga. I bought the book and, after I'd read it, felt for the first time that I didn't need to hide my ambitions as a writer, that when someone asked me what my profession was I could simply say, 'I write'.

I'll feel emboldened by this idea. I'll tell you about my love of Proust, how he's influenced my work. I'll recite his quote about the value of art, how it allows us to make 'the real voyage of discovery in life' as we emerge from ourselves to see the world as someone else sees it. In truth, writing short stories has allowed me to reach out to understand viewpoints different from my own; helped me understand my parents' choices by writing in their voices; find a way of knowing them when doing so in real life has proved impossible.

I'll add that one of my stories allowed me to comprehend how someone might feel living with a temperamental artist, and I'll blush. That story was written so I could understand how you might've lived with my 'writerly' moods, my arrogance and my desire to live beyond the rules. Still, I don't know if you'll read my collection or if you're simply feigning interest. You always saw my writing as a hobby rather than a serious endeavour.

'Are you nervous about the launch?' you'll ask.

'I'm shitting it. But I guess I've done everything that I can, so if it's meant to be and all that. Will you be about?'

'Yeah, I'll try to come.'

'It's up to you,' I'll reply. 'Have you had much time with Sarah while you're here?'

'We went to the cinema last night. I fed her full of McDonald's and pick-and-mix.'

'How old is she now?'

'She's nearly ten.'

'Christ. Time flies. Claire's nearly three. You should hear her say "Unky Sebastizen".'

'What's she like?'

'She's wild. I was flying back from Dubai with her and Jen and she spent half the flight putting Peppa Pig stickers on my face. You know when you see old lions on TV that have cubs jumping all over them but they don't react. I know how those poor bastards feel.'

'You remember the time we took Sarah to Fota?'

I'll recall the drive to Midleton where your sister lived in a new estate. There were Christmas lights hanging around the front window even though it was nearly March. Inside the bay window Sarah was jumping. The front door opened and Audrey waved. She looked younger than her thirty-three years. She was the head off of you, wearing a pink towel bathrobe, her wet hair pulled back in a headband.

'Thanks for taking her out,' Audrey said, scratching her scalp just above her ear. 'I need to get these lesson plans done.'

'No problem. I like the outfit,' you replied.

'Sure, aren't film stars in their gownies at lunchtime?'

''Tis a fine gownie. Go on. Send that young one out to us.'

Sarah appeared at the door, barely four feet tall.

'Come on you with your oversized novelty head,' you said.

'Shut up you with your skanky pants,' she replied, her voice like a song that was playing too fast.

'What happened your shoes?' Audrey asked.

'I can't find my pink ones.'

'What about your trainers?'

'I need the pink ones.'

Audrey raised her eyebrows and went to find them.

As we drove away you asked Sarah if she'd put on her seat beat, looking in the rear-view mirror. The belt was catching her chin. I smiled, thinking about you as a father and wondering if one day we'd be parents ourselves.

'Have you been to Fota much since…' you'll trail off.

'The odd time,' I'll reply. 'Before Jen and Paul left we brought Claire here a good few times. She loved rolling down those slopes at the back.'

'It hasn't changed at all.'

'No, I don't think it ever will.'

I'll remember the view of the lake on the last day we saw each other; we'd sat on the bench looking out at the lily pads, which were so dense they made the lake look like solid ground. A month had passed since you told me to 'just decide'. I'd written a letter after and you'd been infuriatingly polite in your acceptance of it, comforting me, saying we could still be friends.

'If I could just own this bit I'd be happy,' I said, looking out at the rushes and lilies.

'What about the orangery?'

'I'm sure I could live without an orangery.'

You'd laughed.

'You'd be bored after a week.'

We followed the lackadaisical path that led to the orangery, wandering through a tunnel of willows. The sky turned grey, the shadows on the ground melting into one another. A cool breeze whisked up. I shivered, rubbing the backs of my arms.

'Fuck, when the sun isn't out...'

The garden was transformed into shades of brown and dull green. We walked faster but the few gentle drops turned heavy, splashing hard off the path. Racing across the gravel, we ducked under the swiping branches of the willows and took shelter under a huge sycamore, trapped in the furthest part of the garden, the orangery still a way off. The rain gusted under the canopy, forcing us to shelter close to the trunk.

In the distance the grey patina of rain battled against the trees. Our clothes were soaked, your T-shirt clung against your shoulders and chest. The air had turned cool, its scent altered as the heavy pollens were washed away by the aroma of damp leaves and bark. I looked at you: your wet hair stuck to your cheeks, the blonde strands getting caught in your stubble, your blue eyes heavy and shaded. It felt like fiction.

Though I wanted to kiss you, I pretended to examine the graffiti on the tree trunk. It dawned on me that you and I were still in love and I'd hurt you. It was true what the poems in my Leaving Cert had said, that true love conquered all. In this case our love had survived, continuing without the relationship on which it was based.

'So how was Australia?' you'll ask me.

'I didn't love it like. I dunno, there's something about Ireland, about the weather – I think I must be the first person alive to say I missed the rain.'

'Did you see much of it?'

'Not really. Because of Granddad's funeral, I only got to Sydney and Melbourne before coming back.'

'What did you think?'

'It was good. Though I was in Berlin the week before I went to Australia and, honestly, I think it ruined Sydney for me. We met some amazing people, this one guy in particular, Patrick, who, would you believe, ended up in Sydney then when I was there.'

'Oh.' From your face, I'll know you're wondering if Patrick and I fucked. You'll assume not because I offered his name voluntarily to you. 'It was a pity you had to come back. You might've settled a bit if you were there longer.'

'I suppose. It was one tough year. Thanks for the call that day.'

'Sure you called me.'

'I know. But you listened. I don't know why I had to ring.'

'I know how close you were to your granddad. Wasn't I the same with Nan?'

I'll take a deep breath as emotion rises within me. It's no longer the dangerous grief that followed immediately after the funeral. I'd thought about killing myself and it was, perhaps, the closest I've ever come to doing it. These were not the hysterics of an immature mind, the uncontrolled feelings of childhood still running rampant in young adulthood, but a calm consideration of human existence and thinking in that moment that life wasn't worth the struggle.

Of course, I'll never tell you any of this silliness. I'm sure you'd think it melodramatic. Anyway, I found my answer as to whether or not my life was worth living. It wasn't a resounding yes, but it was a yes nonetheless. I was back writing daily; what I was writing was essentially rubbish, a bad novel that would never be published, but I realised I could never kill myself while I'd a story to write, which meant I'd live to an age when the choice of whether I lived or died would be taken from me.

'I think the storm is after calming,' you said, dragging the wet strands of hair from your cheeks. We slipped out from under the sycamore. The sky remained dull and the rumblings of thunder grew faint. I hoped for a gesture or look from you that might give me a sign, but you were unreadable. We rejoined the path and eventually, between the leaves and branches, I caught a glimpse of the orangery.

The lemon trees inside were heavy with fruit but we didn't stop to examine them. The weather, still temperamental, forced us running up the straight path back towards the house and café.

As we hurried across the lawn, I looked at the magnolias planted around the edges. They'd lost their bloom since our previous visit. The walled garden, where the narcissi had been, was ugly. I wished for the moments of ten minutes previous.

After you dropped me home, I wrote you a new letter. Unlike the first, which had blamed my unhappiness on my childhood, the betrayal of parents and my religious upbringing, this letter confessed that I'd cheated on you and that I'd ended our relationship because I couldn't live with the guilt.

That was three years ago. We are strangers for the most part. Nothing has changed since that stormy day. After that second letter we both went our separate ways.

So our coffees in Fota will never happen. Sometimes life can't be fixed; the best the future can offer is the hope that if something incredible were to happen, you might get your way; though, if you thought about it rationally, you'd know that the 'incredible thing' was actually impossible.

Then again, my dreams are now tangible words on a page. So, in one reality at least, we'll meet at our favourite place and muddle on from there.

SILENCIO

Will's phone vibrates under his shoulder. Pulling it out, he glances at the notification: Oriane has posted a video on his profile. Next to him, a young woman turns on her side. He hopes that she'll wake while he's in the shower and slip away quietly.

He glances at his watch and frowns; it's not like Oriane to contact him first. It's something he's complained about but these complaints have limited effect. Though she is always prompt with her replies she once said that it is rude not to text back quickly, so it's not out of any particular favouritism towards him.

'Morning.' The girl smiles at him; she has a modelish face but thin lips. He began noticing lips after Oriane told him that he had full 'kissy lips' and that she loved kissy lips. Her lips felt good against his the few times he kissed them. Was that why Oriane liked kissy lips, because she had them herself?

'Some night, eh?' Will replies. The girl leans over and kisses him. She has bad breath – even pretty girls get bad breath after sleeping drunk. They fool around; he feels her thin lips and he wonders how long it'll be until she decides to go. He doesn't want to hurt her feelings but Oriane is coming to Dublin and he wants to shower and clean the house so it's like last night didn't happen. Yet he's polite; he slips his head down under the covers so she won't think him rude.

They don't go all the way. His mind is distracted. She showers and he pours her a glass of blueberry smoothie. He thinks about making coffee but that would only delay her longer. They swap numbers before she leaves.

The house is silent and he feels he can, with a few simple steps, be himself again. He turns on his laptop, thinking about Oriane. She told him she'll stay with Sebastian at John's house, though she could change her mind as the evening progresses. She has before. Or he might stay on John's couch beside her. Not that they'd have sex, because John is particular about his apartment and its furnishings. There'd be no 'high-five' in the morning at the sight of a used condom stuck to the sitting room floor.

The video on his wall loads. A girl appears out of a Parisian metro station. She's coy, apologetic.

'I'm so sorry, have you been waiting long? Je suis désolée…'

Scenes of Parisian girls, semi-clad, smoking, thin but eating red meat, are cut between images of Parisian boulevards at night. They look like Oriane – no make-up, skinny jeans, wavy hair and red lips – though these girls seem slightly dirty, their foreheads shiny. Oriane never looks dirty. Wherever she stays, she always brings her hairdryer.

It's an odd video. He does not think the Parisian nightclub is any edgier than his usual Dublin haunts, just because the males have quiffs and wear skinny jeans while the girls are pale-skinned, smoking and complaining about loud Americans. The girls who are dancing look good, though with a sexiness that seems slightly off to him; Will imagines that hidden beneath their pseudo-distressed clothes there's folds of unshaven hair.

He wonders why Oriane has posted the video. It only makes her seem more alien to him, a creature he'll never understand, not to mention possess. Of course, she'd have a quote to describe this detachment, which would transform her annoying distance into something ultimately attractive.

She might even cite Proust. Her best friend ('the husband', as she says) Sebastian read *In Search of Lost Time* and filled her head with rubbish. Will wonders what was wrong with two people simply falling in love and getting on with it, doing normal things like having kids and getting the nicest house within their reach.

The problem is that Sebastian thinks too well of Oriane; Will suspects it's the reason why she was dissatisfied with him. After all, gay men either vilify or worship the women around them, and Will has witnessed Sebastian telling Oriane how special she is. This will be fatal in the long run. She could end up with nothing when Will and all of the other admirers have moved on.

But they haven't moved on yet and this is a more worrying thought. Perhaps Oriane will have her admirers all the way to the end. And he'll be one of them because it is near impossible to get over a girl who won't love him in return.

Oriane has shared the video with Will, Sebastian and John. While she packs, she wonders why the majority of people in her life are men. Sebastian says it is because she is a gay man in a woman's body. It is the perfect combination, he says, to think like a man and be a good-looking woman. It makes her overwhelmingly attractive to both sexes, but to men especially.

She smiles. Sebastian does go on sometimes. She glances at her watch and thinks about lunch. She's surprised that none of the three has replied to her post, though it is likely that Will might be in bed and Sebastian is getting a train. Will John like the video? It isn't the sort of nightclub that he'd like. After all, he didn't like Friday nights in WAR.

Opening a vintage leather medicine bag, she places her

toiletries inside, her Touche Éclat and her hairdryer. She opens her wardrobe, wondering what she might wear. Nearly all her clothes are charcoal, cream and navy, as she dislikes bright colours. There's space in the wardrobe because she buys very little; however when she does buy, it tends to be expensive. Inspired by Daphne Guinness, she has never regretted this sort of selective spending because she's slowly built up a collection of clothing that people admire.

She lifts out her eyeliner, a shimmering grey from Chanel that has lasted forever. Leaning close to the mirror, she pulls down her lower lid, darkening the inside of her lashes. She doesn't like the shadows that are creeping into the corners of her eyes, though she's unsure if it's due to age or hay fever.

She decides it's hay fever. Sebastian told her to get a nasal spray. She hasn't yet, nor has she taken the packet of vitamins he bought for her. She knows she's terrible at looking after herself. When she and Sebastian lived together, he was a wife of sorts, scolding her to go to bed and making her dinners. He's warned her about her unhealthy habits, saying 'if you die, I'll kill you'. Then again, he looks well on his healthy lifestyle. They both look younger than their ages. But she didn't enjoy her twenty-fifth birthday; she hates her birthdays, especially those that end in odd numbers, without quite knowing why. And she knows her twenty-seventh is fast approaching.

A notification appears on her phone. It's a response from Will.

'Nice vid.'

Of course he doesn't get it. It is because he doesn't understand the video that she can never fall in love with him. Any love Will claims to have for her will always feel artificial, being based on ignorance. Will only understands her nice side, the part that resembles normality. This other side that remains in Paris, rebellious and youthful, she does not feel ready to give up even if it leads to disaster.

Sebastian understands the whole of her, the two sides. But he is a writer; he sees the world as words, as ideas. Every event in their lives is linked to a line, a text, a piece of dialogue or a song lyric. He would be blind if it weren't for the texts around him, as people and events are only explicable through their links to fiction.

Oriane smiles, remembering the time they were lost in East Berlin. She'd reached for her guidebook only for him to exclaim, 'Throw away your Baedeker, Lucy!' and their predicament was transformed into something to be relished when seen from the perspective of *A Room with a View*.

Oriane lifts a pair of AllSaints heels from the bottom of the wardrobe and places them into the leather bag. She's worn them on previous nights in Dublin and no one seems to mind. And Vivian Westwood said to 'choose well and buy less', which validates her own theories on clothing. She looks forward to seeing John and his beautiful apartment. John is different to her in many respects; essentially they are friends because Sebastian is linked to the both of them. Yet John is funny and a good conversationalist. He is the perfect host, with good manners, a generous nature and a perpetually well-stocked fridge.

Oriane glances at her watch, realising she'll have to catch the next bus if she's to arrive in Dublin at the same time as Sebastian's train reaches Heuston Station. She and Sebastian have told the others that they'll arrive in Dublin later than they actually plan to. They want some time alone together to talk about things that are not secret, yet not appreciated by the others. Sebastian has described their friendship as perfect, reminding him of Montaigne's essays; he's assured

Oriane that the only things he's never told her are things he has forgotten because they're unimportant.

This type of sentiment is typical of him. He lives hard and feels too much. His troubled yet optimistic nature is one of the reasons she loves him. Around him, life is heightened, caught between total discipline and possible chaos. He was probably right when he proclaimed that he'll either live to thirty-six or one hundred. There'll be no half measures.

Oriane's phone beeps and, as if on cue, it's a message from Sebastian. He's on the train, making his way northward to Dublin.

Sebastian is happy because he's managed to find four seats and a table together that are empty. The train has taken off so he knows that unless a number of people get on at Limerick Junction he'll be left undisturbed for the trip. Yet it wouldn't really matter if they did; for some reason people avoid sitting beside him on buses and trains. He theorises it's because he looks moody. Once, on a night out, he was told by a drunken stranger that he looked angry when he was simply lost in his own thoughts.

Sebastian blames his lack of sociability around strangers on his writer's temperament. For him, being in a club is like being a deep-sea diver who can swim with the aid of oxygen, but for whom the environment will always be alien. He knows he can traverse a pub or club with alcohol, but it is never an entirely comfortable experience.

Lifting Edith Wharton's *The House of Mirth* from his weekend case, he admires the leather bag. It was bought on a holiday to Amsterdam with an ex-boyfriend. He's happy, knowing that each part of his appearance is perfect, feeling like Lily Bart on the train. He knows that he has little natural taste when it comes to clothing but he's observed the style of his former boyfriends. He's summed up Male Style as, 'if you can hold a brandy glass without looking ridiculous, your outfit is most likely in good taste'. This has meant his clothing in recent times has favoured tweed jackets, traditional fabrics and well-made leather shoes. Cut comes before colour; inspired by Oriane, he's systematically removing all bright clothes from his wardrobe.

Sebastian sneezes. His allergies have flared up in recent days. As he dabs his nose, a sentence comes into his head: 'one of the true pleasures of being ill is exaggerating the symptoms'. It isn't an idea for any particular story he wishes to write but he types it into his phone for future reference. It sounds like something that Oscar Wilde would've said, which he probably did say. Sebastian sighs: it is annoying that other writers have lived before him; it feels like every new idea he has is simply a version of something already written. He only has to search a phrase online to discover his genius is too late.

Glancing down, Sebastian straightens his T-shirt. It's a small size but he knows he has a good body. He feels he doesn't have to apologise for his confidence because seven years of consistent working out is a valid reason for pride. He and John agree on this; in fact, John wears his T-shirts tighter still. John has a brash confidence in himself, a definite certainty with his style that is very different to Sebastian's own ideas, but Sebastian admires his friend's certainty of character compared with his own shifting aesthetic.

Opening his laptop, he connects it to the internet; the light coming in the carriage windows makes it hard to see the screen. Plugging in his earphones, he starts the clip from Oriane. A girl is wearing red lipstick; he understands Oriane's sudden obsession with MAC Ruby Woo. He's reminded of their time in Berlin when they arrived in the city at nine a.m. on the morning of his twenty-fifth birthday. Their eyes were smeared with her Chanel eyeliner from the night before. He can't remember exactly what they were wearing except that it was expensive and distressed looking. At the airport, people stared at them like they were exotic creatures, perhaps famous. The wonderful feeling that they were extraordinary (though fleeting) had the quality of a drug. Even though he'd worked part-time as a model through university, none of those contrived moments of exposure could compare with this accidental moment of possibility.

The video is to promote Social Club in Paris; Sebastian has been there with Oriane. They kissed the same guy that night. Callum was nineteen years old with full kissy lips. There was something invigorating about him, about Social Club, as if youth had its own particular aura and if one got close enough to it, a person could be a teen again, if only temporarily.

Sebastian turns up the volume on his laptop. He knows others in the carriage can hear the tinny beat from his headphones but the louder the music is, the more alive he feels. 'My Name is Skrillex' – the beat of the song raises his heartbeat. He loves music for this immediacy. For in that one moment he does not want to be anywhere else but on a train to Dublin, watching the video and sensing the possibility of the approaching night.

The video ends. He reads the comment that Will has posted and smiles, thinking Will would've been better off not to write anything. Sebastian doesn't understand Oriane's connection to Will beyond his kissy lips (and the beautiful dick that she's told him about) but he theorises that because Oriane is 'wired like a man' she wants a trophy partner, like a modern-day Catherine the Great. However, he does not think Will is a good enough trophy. Will might be tall but he is badly proportioned with a long back and short legs.

Underneath Will's message Sebastian writes 'EPIC – THIS NEEDS KANYE CAPS'. Oriane will understand what he means, as will John. Part of the fun of friendship is speaking in a language of common cultural references, generally involving celebrities. One of his most enduring phrases is 'I was channelling Anna', after a heavy night that ended with him behaving badly. It was easier to joke that he had been possessed by the spirit of Anna Nicole Smith than explain away the embarrassment.

Sebastian glances at his watch, wondering when John will be finished work. He calls John's number. It rings out and he leaves a message.

'Hey John, just wondering will we come directly to the apartment or will we meet you in Busy Feet? Let me know.'

He wonders if John will hear the train. John might realise that he'll be in Dublin earlier than expected, though it is too late to worry. Sebastian re-watches the video.

'If you want to understand the real Paris watch "Inland Empire" by David Lynch in French.'

Sebastian is certain that John would hate all of David Lynch's films. Then again, John has often surprised him. Sebastian never expected John to become one of his closest friends as they are radically different in their tastes. His first interest in John was entirely sexual as John has perfectly symmetrical features and is six foot two. They had sex while on coke and this encounter led to friendship. Many of his gay friendships began in this way because once the sexual tension was removed, a real connection could happen. There are the Grecian precedents, after all; the mythical legends from which these truths have emerged.

They'd never have worked in a relationship; they would've clashed because John is ordered and definite in his views while he is easily swayed by external influences. Sebastian wants to test limits, find alternative ways to live and discover new types of morality. Perhaps it is too much reading, but so many of the rules that he's been reared with seem without foundation, especially those around sex. In this respect, he and John differ most of all; for example, he knows John would hate the idea of threesomes if they were together but as friends he can laugh at Sebastian's recent accounts of his sexual adventures.

Sebastian smiles as he thinks of John's watered plants, his fridge of cream cheese, wine and bacon, and the freshly cleaned carpets. John is Mrs Dalloway. He deserves his content life with his current boyfriend because his choices and behaviour in recent times have not attracted the attention of life's possible calamities.

John arrives home. He's back from Fallon and Byrne where he bought four chicken fillets wrapped in Parma ham along with gratin potatoes and chopped vegetables. He'll get some wine from Tesco when the others arrive. He hopes Sebastian won't arrive with a bottle of vodka or Morgan Spiced and start drinking early. Sebastian's drinking is a delicate balance between good and awful (never in between). Though in recent times it seems the nights of 'channelling Anna' have grown less frequent. Sebastian is happier, it seems. The book deal has calmed him.

John is looking forward to seeing Oriane. He likes Will and thinks he's good for Oriane, if a bit flaky. Will is good because she is better off not being with someone too like her. If a person ends up with someone too like themselves, they have no alternative viewpoint available when things go awry.

He flicks on the stainless steel kettle. He shouts to his flatmate, asking if she wants some tea, though he's not sure if she's home yet. He glances at his phone to see if his boyfriend has messaged and thinks that Michael is good for him for that reason. Though they had their moments in the previous two years, they've both mellowed, each softening the rough edges of the other. They are different enough to challenge each other.

John opens the Brown Thomas bag and lifts out a T-shirt. It's blue with a large D&G logo woven into the left pocket. It's extra-small; his mother thinks he's too vain but all of his friends are vain. Old people are always complaining that his generation is shallow, but didn't they create a country that they thought would be ideal for their children, a place where there were no big problems like war or disease, where the small problems had room to become big ones, like the straightness of one's teeth or the newness of one's jeans? So he's not going to apologise for buying a one hundred and twenty euro T-shirt that is well made and enhances his body.

It's sunny on the balcony, though the shadows of the table are stretching, hitting the dividing wall. John remembers he must water the plants. Sebastian laughed at his gentle tweaking of their pots when he first bought them, wanting them perfectly positioned. He said that John would 'buy the flowers himself', quoting some book he'd read.

John sniffs his shirt. There's a faint smell of Tom Ford For Men but he's been working all day and thinks about having a shower. His phone vibrates. Sebastian has messaged, asking him how his day is going. John can hear the train and wonders if Sebastian and Oriane are in the city already and if they planned it that way. He decides not to ask. Perhaps they want some time together.

Sitting at the breakfast bar, he opens his laptop. There are a number of messages; one is a video from Oriane. He presses play.

It goes on a bit. The music is annoying and disjointed. The vintage clothes, despite the girl's red lips, do not look vintage, rather dirty and old. It reminds him of WAR, full of nineteen-year-olds trying desperately to be cool and failing because being cool requires effortlessness. Why not buy something decent, something from a catwalk, rather than some grubby fur that an old lady probably died in?

Yet the video reminds him of his semester in France five years earlier. He likes the night-time images and he notices the manager of Social Club is good-looking. The video makes him want to go to Paris again, though this is from a feeling of nostalgia rather than a desire to go to Social Club. He remembers the guys he fucked when he lived there and is happy he did fuck them but feels no need to return to that unsteady life again. He loves his boyfriend and sees a different future that makes the video seem pointless.

'*I'm in fucking Paris*,' a topless drunk girl declares in a toilet cubicle. The video is nearly over.

'*I guess you and I don't have the same vices…*' In a hotel bedroom a red-lipped girl sits on a bed, topless, and John wonders why French girls can be topless and yet not look slutty, even with red lips. The image becomes blurred, her lips drawing closer. She says 'Silencio' and the video ends.

He frowns, wondering why a club would be called Silence. It was trying too hard. Yet it attracted Oriane and Sebastian as they still lived like semi-adults, in a constant state of suggestion. They'd say that it was interesting and that being interesting is all that matters.

In a way it is nice not to understand his friends fully. They are supposed to be different, how else would they have anything to discuss? Yet it is difficult to sustain these friends when everyone worth knowing is ambitious and has scattered themselves around the globe in their efforts to succeed. The sad truth of modern life is that they live in a world where neighbours are not friends and friends are not neighbours.

Silencio. Much of modern life is silence for him, for all of them. Even with a boyfriend and a host of people in his life, there are no accidental meetings in the village shop or going to the local bar and chatting to a relative or acquaintance. Friendships have to be valued to survive the simple issue of logistics. Granted, the internet makes it easier post comments on walls and send messages, to challenge the silence. But on the other hand it's easier for him to see the photos of friends' nights out in far-off places, making him all the more aware of things he's missing.

John glances at his watch. He attaches his phone to the portable speakers, feeling the apartment is too quiet. He decides to listen to something that'll lift his mood. He thinks of Sebastian and Oriane and frowns, wondering again if they're already secretly in Dublin.

His phone rings.

'Hi John.' It's Sebastian.

'Hey.' He can hear traffic and rattling china.

'Listen, Oriane and I got in earlier than we thought. We're having a coffee in Busy Feet. Are you able to call in now? Oriane's giving Will a ring, too.'

'Sure.' Though he's smiling, John tries to keep his voice nonchalant.

'Great – how long do you think you'll be? The sun is gorgeous here.'

John says he'll be fifteen minutes and hangs up. He throws on his jacket and tosses the Brown Thomas bag onto the floor of his bedroom, thinking he can shower later. Closing the front door of his apartment, he hops down the steps onto Pearse Street and walks briskly alongside Trinity College.

Though it isn't quite rush hour, the traffic is heavy. People are finishing early, making their way out of the city for the weekend. John checks his phone; the forecast for the weekend is sunny spells and showers. But that could mean anything in Ireland. He looks up at the sky and there are no clouds. He smiles; it could mean a weekend of pure sunshine.

DEMAIN

I know a man-boy called Patrick. He's German and, though twenty-seven, his unlined, sallow skin means he could be mistaken for twenty-two, possibly even twenty. Perhaps if he looked his age I wouldn't be so forgiving of him.

His face is typically German: he has a strong jawline and high cheekbones, though he possesses an element of the exotic, having dark curling hair (cut tight at the sides) that suggests a Turkish or Latin ancestor. Glistening beetle-brown eyes look out from underneath dark, straight eyebrows.

In the beginning I was attracted because he was almost an alien creature. Perhaps if I'd been in Germany longer I would've seen a thousand Patricks but I'd only landed in Berlin SXF a couple of hours beforehand. He was dancing with two guys, one wearing red braces, the other's face striped with lime paint. I asked him if they were his friends. No, he said, they were his boyfriends.

He was high and had been out for three days straight. Yet he showed no symptom of it – no clammy skin or sour smell of sweat. His brown eyes disguised his dilated pupils. He told us he was thirty and I marvelled at how he defied time, sleep and nourishment, reminding me of Dorian Gray.

Finding the club in the industrial estate had been tricky, wandering past broken bottles and dry grass, feeling the first trickle of sweat on my neck from the heat of the sun. I asked Oriane if we were going in the right direction. She checked her phone and nodded, her eyes lighting up. We continued down the broken footpath until a faint thump of base quickened our step. A rectangular monolith of Berghain appeared on our left, the entrance scarred with graffiti. 'Happy twenty-fifth birthday!' Oriane smiled at me. Having got through the 'no normals' door policy, we were greeted by booths, darkrooms, condoms at the bar, straights, gays, topless, rugby players, models, transsexuals – all tempting and repulsive.

Outside, behind the closed shutters of Berghain, the sky was blue, as Sunday afternoon drifted into evening. I was in no mood to talk, thick-headed from a sleepless weekend. The air was heavy with smoke but when the window shutters opened, flooding evening light into the club as the electronic beats reignited, I felt a momentary euphoria.

I watched Patrick; he remained smiling but distant. He flirted with others and kissed his boyfriends, making me irrationally jealous. I walked to the bathrooms, past torn sofas and half-sleeping neon youths. My fingertips touched the chipped concrete wall, greasy with handprints. Slipping past the sinks, I avoided eye contact with a male as I went inside the furthest cubicle. As I closed the door, a sallow hand caught it. It was Patrick.

I smiled and shook my head; he'd kissed others and I didn't want to be a number. So he wandered off and I closed the door. I fiddled with my phone despite having no one to contact, enjoying the fact that in the cubicle I was alone. When I returned to the bar, Patrick appeared to have forgotten the incident and was dancing with Oriane. She swapped numbers with him. I fumbled a goodbye, relieved to leave.

For November it was hot, even for Sydney. I sat in Hyde Park; a breeze caught the spray of the fountain, misting water onto my face. I took Oriane's card of out my bag if only to remind myself of those feelings I'd had in Berlin:

To my dearest ingénu on your '17th birthday' (for the 8th time!)

And what an amazing year it'll be! Master's done and off to sunny Australia for a second summer in one year – how fab! And to be going there for inspiration and experiences, which will energise your body and mind for writing to come, oh S, it's gonna be unreal! Sometimes think we forget how young we are – this is such a brilliant way to make the most of our freedom! I'll miss you so much but when I think of how much this experience of travelling and living on the other side of the world will feed your personal growth and writing...

I smiled at its exuberance. It wasn't that my first six weeks in Sydney had been unpleasant, but there'd been unease. I wasn't as happy as I'd expected to be. This made me curious to see Patrick again, as my memories of that Sunday afternoon in Berghain were vague, not to mention it seemed too big a coincidence that we were both in Sydney.

Truth be told, I was hoping that he'd be interesting in a way I'd discovered Australians were not. I found myself bored by gyms, beaches, house music and barbecues; as a friend said, 'all the Shakespeares were out surfing'. Perhaps I was generalising or simply nostalgic, but Europe became more defined in my mind as my true home, the place that would draw me back before long. I wondered whether I should've paid so much attention to a professor who'd said, 'Go travel, live a little before you write, ideally somewhere you don't know the culture, even better if you don't know the language'. Of course, I'd argued with him regularly; he'd called my work naïve.

I saw Patrick's red and black T-shirt from a distance. I stood up and gave him a loose hug. He looked no different, still sallow and youthful as I remembered. He spoke of Berlin, his going-away party and his current life in Sydney. I didn't want to tell him that I'd been dating Paul since my own arrival. Paul was a different part of me, a side that liked chart music, wore Diesel jeans and T-shirts from high-street stores.

I slipped Paul's name into the conversation but Patrick seemed unconcerned. Instead he'd new music for me to listen to, fresh from Berlin. I thought I liked it, the minimalist dance beats, while Patrick danced unashamedly outside the Queen Victoria Building, catching his reflection in a shop window. We both paused and gazed at ourselves, enjoying the transgression of public vanity. I laughed; we were more alike than I'd thought.

Patrick was staying in Sydney for two months, living in a friend's apartment in Pott's Point. It was an old building that required him to come downstairs to open the outside gate. He was barefoot, something I didn't approve of, and was wearing a T-shirt with the sleeves torn off; it read 'I heart Berlin', except the heart was exploded ink. I was conscious of my own clothes, that I looked perfectly acceptable. I was not Berlin.

The apartment was compact – two bedrooms and a balcony that faced onto a quiet street. A tree was growing out front, its leaves blocking views of the harbour. It was balmy and the street below was lit by occasional bursts of low-key lighting, reminding me of a comic book.

Patrick poured me a glass of wine.

'Are you hungry?' he asked, 'I haven't eaten since three hours.' I said I wasn't but he made me a salad anyway.

'How are you spending your time?' I asked.

'I went to the beach, the Taramara – you know it?' he replied. I nodded enthusiastically. Taramara was the only beach on the eastern strip that interested me: it was small, sheltered by cliffs; reminiscent of an Irish beach, only with sunshine. Patrick asked about my job; I was working in the Central Business District and was already bored of the shirts and ties, long hours, and repetitiveness. I never lasted in a job for long, constantly seeking ways to return to university.

'You heard much from your family since you've been here?' Patrick asked.

'Yes, a good bit from my sister, and I try to ring my granddad a bit.' I remembered my going-away meal, the circle of relations in Courbett Court restaurant, my older sister picking the anchovies out of her salad, my grandfather asking my aunt Kate if she'd order him jelly and custard, and the notable yet unsurprising absence of my parents.

Patrick lifted out a packet of tobacco and rolled a cigarette, licking the edges of the papers, sealing in the blackened leaves. Using an oven lighter, he lit it, seating himself on the balcony ledge. I frowned, thinking about the drop behind him.

'You hear from your friend Oriane?' he asked.

'Yes, we chat every few days; she saw me off at Dublin airport,' I said. And I realised how final my journey to Sydney was and I wondered what it'd be like to return after saying so many goodbyes, if I'd blush as I thought about the failure of my trip.

I asked him about his life in Sydney. He admitted that he'd begun a memoir. I asked to read it but it was written in German. Opening his laptop, he translated the first couple of sentences: 'I am Patrick and I am twenty-seven years old…' Like the music he listened to, it was stripped of all fuss. Very

German, I thought. I'd finished my glass of wine though Patrick had barely started his. He read on; I stopped him when he mentioned a heart operation.

'Is that true?' I asked. He nodded.

'It's a defect since birth. I had operations growing up; part of my aorta is fake.'

'But the drugs?'

'I know. But you've got to live. I was always protected. My parents and sisters… you can't play safe always.' There was a pause before he said: 'are you writing since you are here?'

I shook my head.

'Between the working and the drinking,' I laughed. 'I'm taking some time out, doing a bit of living.'

He nodded, changing the subject, complaining about the price of drugs in Sydney, the lack of ketamine or a proper electro scene. Yet he'd discovered a club night, The Electric Carnival, which I agreed to go to.

We walked into the spare bedroom and Patrick slid open the mirrored wardrobe door. His friend who owned the apartment apparently had money; inside were rows of unworn designer clothing: jumpers designed with curling knots and twisted seams, skinny jeans, braces, T-shirts with stretched necks, and perfectly over-washed prints. Patrick began trying them on, encouraging me to do so. He picked up his camera and one by one I tried different tops, my uncertainty fading.

The Electric Carnival turned out to be only middling. The best part was the expectation that I felt in the taxi as we arrived at the venue, both dressed in clothes stolen from the wardrobe. In the back seat, I could see the silver paint streaked across Patrick's cheek below the glint of his eyes.

That night I drank to ignore the fact that though the event

was alternative in look – a host of leather bras and dreadlocks – it was a false Berlin. The music drifted towards pop and Patrick found it uninteresting. He grew flustered when I talked about Paul; he hadn't heard me mention him in Hyde Park. Perhaps it was a language thing.

We attempted a second night out but with similar results. Had it been in Europe, had there been more drugs, things might've turned out differently. I left Patrick talking to a journalist in a smoking room, while an unknown DJ played inside. Walking along Crown Street, I made my way towards Paul's apartment, feeling sober and increasingly apathetic.

I didn't see Patrick again for a couple of weeks. I sensed that I might've been relegated to the realm of uninteresting. Instead, I hung out with my Irish friends. Though it went against my plans for Sydney, recreating my old Dublin life was fun and easy. I drank too much and spent my days hungover, gazing vacantly at my computer screen at work.

Lying on the front deck of the small but sleek boat, I closed my eyes and felt the first waves of pleasure from the pill trace their way under my skin. The sun warmed me; I wondered for a moment about the tan lines, for though I was essentially topless, the navy braces curved around the outside of my nipples.

'Jez,' I said, 'I'm getting a bang off of those. Did you take a whole or a half?'

'I took a whole one. There's a bit of a buzz all right.' Next to me on the deck was Michelle, who worked in the booth beside me in the call centre. In the background I could hear Basement Jaxx. I opened my eyes; across the front of the boat a mix of Irish, Scottish and Spanish were strewn, drinking and sunning themselves, all dressed in variations on a sailor theme. One of the Scottish girls next to me was rubbing sun cream onto her shoulders; her saucer-eyes were partly disguised behind large sunglasses.

'Thank God we're not stuck in that shithole,' Michelle said. 'I couldn't give two shites about those fecking orders.' Michelle avoided dealing with the really difficult customers by cutting their call short and memorising their number, so that when they dialled back in she could avoid answering.

I realised that I was clenching my jaw. I relaxed it, glad that I was finally calm. There was something alien about these social environments that I would never truly enjoy till my first pill or second drink. I'd hover on the edge of groups not sure of what to say, and undecided if this lack of connection was a good thing or not. Even saying happy birthday to the girl – whose birthday this trip around Sydney Harbour was for – was forgettable when compared to the 'Happy birthday, ya big ride' that one of the other Irish guys roared as they pretended to dry-hump her. Though I knew she wasn't that interested anyway; my invite was more to make the space look full than from any particular desire by her to know me.

However, I liked talking with Michelle about how crap our jobs were. I enjoyed taking a deep drag of the joint as it was passed along the row of bodies in the sun. And I thought perhaps this was the type of adventure that my professor had been speaking of and that for now, instead of thinking, it was better to be living. When I was old, I could always write about being fucked off my head on a boat in Sydney Harbour and find something meaningful in it.

'So tell me this, I saw some pictures of you as Lady Gaga,' Michelle said. 'You've a good aul arse.'

I smiled; I'd been to a 'Life's a Drag' birthday party back in Dublin and had been proud of the fact that I was one of the earliest 'Little Monsters' to dress as Gaga, complete with knickers, leather jacket and disco stick. I'd laughed at the attention walking up George's Street, the whistles that were not (as I'd feared) threatening but in good humour; I'd been surprised to discover how liberal the city truly was. However, as the night progressed, I'd got progressively drunker and back at an after-party my long blond wig had to be thrown away after I vomited onto it.

'It was a great night,' I said.

'So I hear you do some writing,' Michelle said. She swallowed twice, her chin tensing. 'What kind of stuff?'

'I'm not doing anything at the moment.' I swallowed. 'Fecking call centre taking over my soul.'

'Jez. No wonder Sharon (Sharon was a forty-year-old who'd been working in the call centre a decade; she weighed about seven stone) is off her game with speed.'

'Speed?'

'Look at her. It's a wonder she's any back teeth left…'

At eleven p.m., slightly sunburnt, I walked back to my apartment. My hair was knotted after diving into Sydney Harbour; even through the haze of alcohol and pills, I'd wondered how likely it was that I'd drown as I leapt off the boat. I'd kissed three of the party guests, two girls and one of the guys. Not that it mattered, as most things seemed excusable on pills. I wondered if Paul would find out, though I'd found a wall growing within myself against him, a barrier that'd killed my desire. It might have been what is described as 'falling out of love', though I wasn't sure if it was that or a general disconnection from my life in Sydney when I wasn't drunk or high.

Opening my bedroom window, I felt cool air flow in. My rucksack slipped from my shoulders onto the floor. As I picked my phone off the dresser, I smiled, thinking that I could never be a true rebel or anarchist because an anarchist would've brought their phone to the party and not cared if it ended up at the bottom of the harbour.

There were four missed calls and two messages. Blinking a number of times in the vain hope of moistening my dry eyes, I opened the history and saw all of the calls were from my sister's Irish number. Both messages said the same thing: 'Can you call me asap x'.

I hesitated, wondering if it'd be best to wait till the morning before making the call but I knew I wouldn't sleep without knowing. My family had been so rarely absent of drama in the first quarter of my life, it seemed unsurprising that it would continue and that the perfect image in my head of eating dinner together in Courbett Court would inevitably change.

I dialled her number and it was answered immediately.

'Seb, I've been trying to call you all day.'

'Sorry, I was off at that harbour party.'

'Jesus…'

'What's wrong?'

'It's Aunty Kate. They…' She paused a moment; I could hear her swallow. 'They've found cancer.'

'Fuck,' I said. For a moment I was unable to find any other words. So I said fuck three more times in different volumes and tones.

'What are they doing?' I asked. 'Are they starting chemo?'

'They can but…'

'But what?'

'They say it's too late.' I could hear her voice break.

'What about Granddad?' I asked. An idea of him dying crossed my mind, though I tried to ignore it.

'He doesn't know. She doesn't want to say anything to him yet.'

'Fuck,' I said again. 'I have to get home.'

'No, no, no. She didn't want me to tell you yet; there are a few months. She doesn't want to ruin your time.'

'Ruin my time…' The idea that I would be at her funeral, not as at some vague distant point in the future when she was an old woman, but within a year, made my eyes sting.

'Just hang on till the New Year,' Stephanie said. I could hear her blow her nose. 'There's no rush. She said she really doesn't want to ruin your time. Honestly… honestly… there's a bit of time. Don't rush, at least not yet.'

Patrick opened the door; his hair was different, the sides shaved tight so his scalp was visible. The top remained uncut, curls falling heavily onto his forehead. As I passed through the sitting room, I noticed a canvas on the floor with a faint sketch on it.

'What are you drawing?' I asked.

'I don't know. I'll just see what happens. You can have it when it's done.'

I was flattered, though I sensed he created things every day – photographs, lyrics and stories – all of them disposable.

'How was your boat party the other week?' he asked. 'I saw the pictures online.'

'Oh, it was fun. It was… yeah. Good fun.'

Patrick introduced me to his friends who were sitting out on the balcony. After twenty minutes, I wondered why he'd invited guests who were not young, good-looking, talented or fun. The person with the most promise was a gay priest but even he, with his affectations, became exhausting. Patrick was wasted in such company, unless all he was looking for was to be admired.

It was after midnight when the others left. Patrick asked about Paul; I told him that it had ended. I finished a large glass of wine, asking him about his hair. He said he'd shaved it himself.

'Cut mine,' I said. 'Do whatever the fuck you want with it.'

'What do you want me to do?'

'I don't care.'

I sat topless on the edge of the bath while he slid the trimmers over my head, the locks falling around me. I was aware that the skin on my torso was white and that I hadn't worked out as much as I would've liked. In vain I tried to stroke the pieces of cut hair from my shoulders, but they stuck to the skin. I gazed at the small bathroom mirror, watching him cut. He was deep in concentration; I was disappointed that he was being so careful.

'So what do you think?' he asked.

'Yeah, it looks great,' I said. The style was to a high finish, close at the sides, heavier through the top. Yet the sides were not as tight as his own, simply a tame copy.

We sat on the couch with the balcony doors open, taking photographs of ourselves, which he altered on his laptop so they appeared as Warhol prints and comic book caricatures. I was less photogenic, though in all the photographs he was frowning. I leaned in and kissed him and it felt perfect. Not just because he was a good kisser (I'd kissed plenty of those without feeling anything like that). Rather because it was a sad kiss; I wanted to go further but he wouldn't allow it. He said we would meet in a day or two.

I received a text from him cancelling our date. His daily run had left him breathless, his heart was acting up and he needed to rest.

As I took off my shirt and trousers, slipping into a pair of shorts, I worried about the man-boy alone in his apartment with a damaged aorta, thinking of him dead on the balcony. I dialled his number. The phone rang out. Eventually, after numerous calls, he answered and told me that he'd gone to meet someone else.

'I get it. I'm not your type,' I said.

'It's not that. It's just I'm fucked up. You've no idea.' Yet he was twenty-seven and there came a point when someone could no longer use their past as an excuse, when they graduated from 'fucked up' to just being an asshole. I deleted his number.

Sitting on the bed, I turned on my laptop. I opened Gaydar first, scanning down the rows of photographs, frowning at the gym-acquired bodies. I'd long given up the illusion that going out and fucking one of them would bring me happiness; I'd tested that idea too many times before without any sort of result. What I wanted was to be home, or at least feel 'home', as I had done during my Master's, when I'd experienced that sense of certainty that I was on the right path.

I received a chat invite from *Mad for Fun 83*

'Hi ;) what you after sexy?'

I smiled, looking at his profile. He was wearing a rugby

jersey in his profile pictures, though one of the others showed him topless on a beach, the folds of his black shorts hinting at the outline of his cock. He was looking directly at the camera, thumbs up, which made me wonder if he was a bit of a tool.

Yet the jersey reminded me of GAA guys, masculinity and sweat, and it seemed irrelevant whether or not he was smart. It didn't really matter if it was all an illusion; I wanted to get naked with him and I didn't give a shit whether or not it made me happy or fucked me up further.

'Just seeing what's happening. Chats. Odd hookup,' I answered.

'Sounds good to me ;) Fancy some odd hookup tonight? You single? Attached?'

'Single. You accom? What you into?'

'All on my own. Vers here. Looking for vers guy.'

'Nice one. Same. Nothing like flipflop.'

'Sweet. Luke here btw. Wanna call by? You like group fun?'

I took his address and sat on the bed. I looked at my phone, thinking about Patrick and Paul. I could feel my cock pushing against my jeans and I sensed the split between my desire and something else.

I smiled, remembering the words of Oscar Wilde about being able to resist 'anything but temptation', and I wondered was it almost essential as a writer to do stupid things, the things that normal people didn't do, so that I might have something to say. Then I realised, writer or no writer, I wanted to fuck a hot guy. I put on my trainers.

We fucked in Luke's open plan apartment and like most sex, it was far better in my imagination than it actually was. His cock wasn't as big as I'd hoped and he kissed roughly, trusting his tongue into my mouth. Worse still, he had no awareness that good sex, even if entirely casual, had to have the illusion of possibility; he was as dumb as the thumbs-up in his photograph.

His apartment door closed behind me and I glanced at my watch, realising that only an hour had passed. After I'd cum, there was nothing about him that I found attractive; I felt no need to wait fifteen minutes for us both to get aroused again. I knew I'd rather be at home vacantly browsing the internet, watching South Park and occasionally masturbating, using up time till I fell asleep. I walked down the flights of stairs to the building entrance and I thought disdainfully of the photographs on Luke's profile, that were of him but exceptionally flattering versions, realising that from the moment he opened the door I didn't find him attractive and what had transpired was a mere politeness, a 'well, I've made the journey so we might as well fuck'.

As I neared my own apartment, walking through the leafy suburbs of Elizabeth Bay, I thought about my Australian flatmates and I hoped they were out, for even having to offer the customary greeting to them felt like a burden.

My phone beeped and for a second I wondered if it was Patrick. It was Luke.

'Fuckin hot man. Ya didn't need to run off. Come back for seconds if ya like.'

I rolled my eyes, deleting it. I took a deep breath, asking myself what the fuck was I doing.

I sat on the bed, opening the laptop and rubbing my balls, as I'd not wiped off all the lubricant in my rush to leave Luke's bedroom. I hoped that when Skype opened, Oriane would be online, as she was the only person whom it was never an effort to talk to.

She wasn't, probably in the university library, checking out guys across the balconies, as I'd done with her previously. It had been fun then, when we were both undergraduates; but now at twenty-five rather than twenty-two, being that frivolous and acting like teenagers had, for the first time, an element of tragedy – the tragedy of trying to be younger than I was.

I opened the internet browser and I checked Gaydar; Luke was online again, most likely looking for more 'fun' with other guys. I closed the window, opening Facebook. I had four notifications; one was a message from Paul. I saw the opening words, 'So do you still want to meet some poin…' I didn't open the message, deciding I'd answer in the morning.

Two of the notifications were 'likes' to photographs that I'd posted of my trip to the Blue Mountains with Paul a month previous. There was also an invite from the guys at work, wondering if I wanted to go to a Goon and Coon party. I accepted the invite, hesitantly wondering if the night would be the same as all the other nights in Sydney: getting pissed and listening to music off somebody's MacBook, before wandering to Oxford Street and drinking schooners of beer till I forgot how I'd got home, waking up next to a half-eaten burger from Oporto, hoping that a shower would make me able for work in the call centre.

The final notification was a link that Oriane had posted on my wall.

'Irish Gaga, you need to see this,' she'd written below. I smiled and pressed play on the video.

Gaga was wearing a black bra under a jacket, her make-up

in the style of a nineteen fifties pin-up. She sipped from a china teacup while a London hipster interviewed her. He seemed nervous, though I found his pretension of a moustache irritating, reminded of the song 'Being a Dickhead's Cool'. Gaga asked a girl behind the camera if her circular-framed sunglasses were on straight.

'In short, I don't give a fuck what anyone else thinks,' Gaga said. She spoke confidently, the language slipping in and out of registers, sometimes flippant, ironic, self-aware, yet other times thoughtful, reminding her audience that underneath the lipstick, behind the whimsical china cup, was someone who was certain they had something worth saying.

'I love Rilke. It's no secret that I live my life in utter submission and loyalty to Rilke,' she said when asked about her influences.

Watching the thirteen parts of the interview, I noticed how often she mentioned Rilke. I'd never read any of his work and searched online, through Wikipedia, until I found an online version of *Letters to a Young Poet*.

Paris. February 17, 1903

Your letter arrived just a few days ago. I want to thank you for the great confidence you have placed in me...

As I began to read the first letter, I smiled, wondering how the poet would have felt if he knew that one day his letters would be accessible online, more freely available than even his poems. I skimmed over the first couple of paragraphs, which I felt verged on sentimentality. I frowned at his condemnation of art criticism. Yet halfway through the third paragraph I paused to reread a sentence:

Go into yourself. Find out the reason that commands you to write; see whether it has spread its roots into the very depths of your heart;

confess to yourself whether you would have to die if you were forbidden
to write. This most of all, ask yourself in the most silent hour of your
night: must I write?

I inhaled and as I read my heartbeat rose. Years later I
would understand the experience through the words of
Proust, that a writer's work is an 'optical instrument' through
which a reader can discern within himself what he might
never have seen without the text. As I read each line that
followed, I wished I had the letters in hard copy, for I found
I wanted to underline quotes, to write notes in the margins,
to spend time with these ideas. Line after line I read truths
that mirrored and finally vocalised my own inner truth that
I'd neglected since coming to Australia.

Within twenty minutes, the fact that I'd fucked an idiot an
hour earlier seemed irrelevant. The fucking didn't feel like an
hour ago but years in the distant past. Now that the cause of
my dissatisfaction was becoming apparent, those feelings I'd
experienced while on Gaydar disappeared. It was not Patrick,
or anything around me that was the problem. The problem
was within; my need to create was being starved. Australia
was not nurturing me for some epic work in the future; rather
I was avoiding the certainty of my vocation. To remain not
writing felt like dying; not that I was dying immediately, rather
withering inside.

I realised what had drawn me to Australia was not
adventures to one day write about, for I'd always been certain
that I had something to say wherever I was, even when I was
living in a remote village in North Cork. I needed no grand
tour for inspiration; that was innate. What had brought me
here was the fear of what to do next after finishing university,
a fear that pervaded most of the travellers around me.

There could be no waiting to write. At the end of the day, if all I had to talk about were the challenges of finding one's place in the world, then that would have to do. Because as Socrates said, 'the unexamined life is not worth living'. Nor was the life waiting for the examination to begin. If my writing was a 'must', as Rilke said, I would make it my first priority, no matter what the eventuality. Even if people thought my work was shit. For if the worst possible outcome was that my work remained unread on a disintegrating hard drive, would it be so very bad if the simple process of writing had given my life meaning?

We met at Coco Cubano in King's Cross. Flags and pictures of Che Guevara hung from the wooden wall panels. A glassless window looked out on the street at people travelling in and out of the neighbouring metro entrance. Patrick was sitting outside, wearing a leather band with a shark's tooth around his neck. I wore a wine-coloured T-shirt, Diesel jeans and brown Paul Smith shoes with wine laces.

On the table, a plastic bag wrapped around a canvas; he pushed it in my direction. I admired the painting's simplicity, asking about his inspirations. He shrugged and said he didn't know, that it 'just came from him'. I asked him was it a self-portrait. He denied it.

'Your message mentioned that you're leaving Sydney,' I said. Patrick nodded. He was flying to the Philippines to see his two boyfriends who were living on one of the islands. The conversation remained light. I spoke of a short story that I was working on and gave him a book that contained a piece I'd previously written. I decided not to tell him about my aunt, or that I would be flying home the following week.

There didn't seem any point.

Yet I felt like my old self again; when I talked it was not to impress him but to express myself. We chatted until I realised I was late to meet Michelle for some goodbye drinks. Finishing my coffee, I spoke briefly about Berlin, the place I'd seen as a possible solution to normal life. It, like Patrick, was an 'other' that would always fascinate.

We parted and I realised I'd forgiven him and that it was really a forgiving of myself for my own blunders Yet one side of me wanted to save him, seeing an unfocused man-boy who was travelling on to something else, and who'd probably leave that eventually also.

Later, when I returned home, I unwrapped the painting, flattered at the idea that I now owned a piece of art dedicated to me. Yet I knew it was not me he'd drawn. Though he'd denied it, it was undoubtedly a self-portrait. The shiny beetle eyes were unmistakeable. The figure was shouting; its face was lined with pain and frustration. Written above its head was a word in French: *Demain*.

I sighed; Patrick was right to turn me down, if only for his own sake. If this was to be his 'tomorrow', I would've tried to protect him. And for that, he would never have forgiven me.

I smoothed my hand over the art deco-inspired cover. The plane taxied on the runway and I knew in nine hours I'd be in Hong Kong and in twenty-four I'd be landing in Ireland, with my sister waiting for me at the airport. Opening the first two pages, I read the inscription for the third time:

To my dearest Sebastian,

May these letters continue to inspire you every day, reinforcing that passion within for your art. Will always remember that first passage you read to me over the phone, about the crucial need to look inward and ask ourselves must I write, create…?

Love you so much,

Oriane

The book had arrived in the post the morning previous. I smiled, happy that I'd see her in only a matter of days. And though apprehensive, I knew the months to come with my family were the real life, not the sort that needed to be found through travel. They'd be the kind that deserved to be lived and would inevitably be written about.

Everything seemed manageable with my new commitment to my work. At the end of the day, my saviour would never be 'somewhere' or 'someone'; it would always be me. And this realisation, like all realisations, was not an end point but simply the beginning of a new journey, a new way of living.

Some Sort of Beauty

I knock on the farmhouse door. The paint is half flaked off, a mint colour. It was probably emerald once but the sun has been hitting it for goodness knows how long. I've a few butterflies; I always do when it comes to this. I don't think I'll ever quite get the hang of it, as I wouldn't be the performing type. But this is life-saving work and you won't find me going against the Bible.

I'm standing with Christine; she's from Liverpool and is wearing a flowery dress with a red jacket. It looks like a Laura Ashley thing, roses and leaves on it, like what Susan wears. Christine's been a special pioneer for donkey's; I remember her knocking on my door all those years back in a similar sort of a dress.

We're taking it in turns to talk to people. It's her go and she's taking a *Watchtower* and an *Awake!* out of her bag. She's got a confidence that I never had with this sort of thing. I couldn't do the sixty hours a month that she does, out knocking on doors every day. I tried pioneering all right and I did manage the hours but I was wrecked from it. With a wife, three girls, work and then preaching on top, I was shattered. It wasn't hard physically but just being on edge for that many hours a day – it took the wind right out of my sails.

An old woman answers the door. She's holding a carton of milk.

'Good moornin, my nayme's Christine and this is Paul. We're just callin around to the howses in the area, askin people what they think abowt the news that…'

I look at the woman's frowning face. I'm not sure if it's due to concentration or suspicion. I wonder if Christine's Liverpudlian accent makes her wary. Maybe she can't understand her.

'Who are ye now?' the woman says.

'We're Jehovah's Witnesses… from Ballymacarther,' I reply.

The old lady stares at me; I hope my Cork accent will relax her. I notice the smell of stale milk. It's very different to sour milk; it's a dull smell from just being on a farm.

'Ye're Jehovah's. No, no… I'm happy as I am…' The door begins to close.

'It's greais that yous have your owen faith…' Christine replies but it's too late. The door clicks shut. Christine puts the magazines in her bag. We walk to the car and return to our conversation about her children, Alex, who's eleven, and Becky, who's sixteen. Sometimes it feels like the brief conversations we have with people are almost interruptions from our own chats.

'He's been practicin all week,' Christine says. It's Alex's first Bible reading on Thursday at the Kingdom Hall. It's a tough enough passage from Proverbs. I don't know if I could've done it at his age, though these last few years I've been conducting the Watchtower Study every Sunday. I've come a long way with the brothers since those early days when I had the Harley. That's why I wear long-sleeved shirts; I don't think I'd be much of a Witness if people saw my tattoos.

'Any luck?' Marion says, as we open the car doors and hop in. Paul is texting on his phone beside her but she's sitting forward, all eager. She's in her early thirties and I'm not sure if she's decided to stay single so she can keep pioneering, or if it's the other way around. She has long loose hair and just a bit of eye make-up, a great-looking girl but I'd say the young lads find her a bit intense. Didn't Paul's eyes roll back in his head when he got paired with her this morning, but they were the only two left. He's twenty-one but he's like a teenager with the things he does to his beard – goatees and side-burns like they're drawn on with a pen. The top button of his shirt is open and his tie an inch down from his neck; it's another act of rebellion, I suppose.

'She didn't want to talk,' Christine replies.

'Really? She used to take the magazines before,' Marion adds. I wonder did the old woman take the magazines because of Marion's sheer persistence, as an attempt to get rid of her. I can't imagine her sitting down after Nuacht or Fair City and opening a *Watchtower*. She's more likely to reach for her rosary. Then again, you never know. People change. I certainly did.

I drive out of the yard, turning onto the narrow road. I know I should try and snap out of my mood. It's been a tough month but the brothers and sisters have been very supportive with all their cards and calls. A few dropped in dinners, too, huge plates of pasta and rice for the microwave. I don't think they expected me to be out this morning but I needed to clear my head and keep busy.

'We should take the next left,' Paul says. He's looking at the Ordnance Survey map. We've covered three roads so far. There are four other cars out this morning; about twenty brothers and sisters witnessing on roads close by.

'How've you got on so far?' I ask.

'Grand,' Paul says. 'I've placed four. Marion placed about ten, of course.'

Marion smiles; her ability to keep people from closing their doors is legendary, getting around those 'conversation stoppers', as they're called at the ministry school. It's all nerve, being able to ask 'What doesn't interest you? Is it religion in general?' when people inch the door towards the latch.

If only they knew what it was like. There's a great camaraderie between all us Witnesses. Whenever something goes wrong you've great support. Didn't I clean up my own life something unbelievable because of them? I remember the village thinking that the Witnesses had paid me to convert but that was a load of rubbish. Sure, after cutting out the fags and giving up the booze, I could kit the house out, not a bother. It was the Witnesses that got me my girls too. If they hadn't vouched for me, I'd say she'd have got custody. But it was clear in the courtroom, hands down, that I'd got myself together. The judge was never going to give them to her, with her denim mini and stink of cigarettes.

I'd say I'd be dead if it wasn't for the Witnesses. Sure, she'd run off and there was me with three girls, raising them and trying to make a living at the same time. The sisters were great, minding the girls when I needed a bit of help, making dinners and all sorts of things. Then there were the clothes, the hand-me-downs. Granted, you wouldn't see as much of that these days but back in the eighties no one had a penny. You wouldn't have got by otherwise.

Paul's phone beeps.

'The others are going for a coffee up at the Bluebell Woods.'

'Will we do one more?' Marion asks.

'The houses aren't going anywhere,' Paul replies, attempting a laugh. Good-humouredness is the only way to deal with Marion's rampant enthusiasm. If you got wound up every time she said something, you'd drive yourself mad. She always gets her own way anyhow.

We pull up outside the next house and Paul and Marion get out. I watch as they walk up the gravel driveway to the new bungalow. The garden is still being landscaped, a big pile of dirt at one end of the front lawn, though it isn't so much a lawn as a field.

'How's Claire getting on?' Christine says.

Claire is my eldest. Personality-wise we're very different; she's too like her real mother. Then again, she's the only one of the three who ever gave me any bit of respect.

'She seems all right, though Siobhan's taking it bad.' I feel I can mention Siobhan even though she doesn't go to any meetings, because she's married and hasn't been disfellowshipped.

'It's so hard on ye aull. Witness or no Witness, Evelyn was still family. You really are doin so so well, aull of ye. If there's anythink we can do...'

I smile, turning away, looking at a haggard rosemary bush at the edge of the lawn. I was on a job when I heard, fixing a roof up Ballyporeen direction. Claire rang me. I'd a mouthful of nails. I could barely understand a word with the wind.

'Evelyn was hit...' Her voice broke off. I didn't really process it at first. Evelyn had been walking home one evening and was killed by a drunk driver.

The car doors open.

'No answer,' Marion sits in. She sounds disappointed.

'Time for coffee?' I say, rousing myself. Paul looks happy for the first time all morning.

I pull up next to a red Citroen and silver Fiat Punto at the entrance to the woods. I step out of the car and stretch my arms, enjoying the feel of the sun on my face. The Bluebell Woods is one of my favourite places to stop for a coffee. It's the kind of place that the more you visit it, the more you like it. Over the years, I've come to realise you can almost set your watch by the arrival of the bluebells, great carpets of them down at the river's edge.

I glance over at the Punto: the young brothers and sisters are sitting inside and I can hear music playing. Paul walks over to the car and he's greeted loudly. He sits inside and the door closes. Marion sighs. I smile at her.

'They're only young once.'

Her expression doesn't change. I think she finds it hard to understand this aura of begrudging that the young ones give off. But at least they're out on the ministry. There aren't many other religions that can say that about their young people. In time, they'll mellow out and become fine brothers and sisters. I've seen it happen over and over again.

'Would you likhe a coffee?' Christine asks; she opens the boot and lifts a flask and a packet of biscuits out of a wicker basket. I tell her one spoon of sugar, taking a ginger nut and leaning against the car door. I watch the trees, still wet from the last shower.

If you can forgive the rain, there's no country like Ireland. I lived in England after Susan and I married, but I'd a hankering for home that brought us back after a couple of years. Even the air over there was not the same; I'd get mad allergies from the pollution – sore eyes and a runny nose. The girls settled all right; I don't remember them having any trouble with the new schools at all. Sure, no one would bully Evelyn anyhow.

'There's your coffee,' Christine says. 'I'm gonna head ovah to the others, you comin?'

I follow Christine. At the river's edge, I see a group of brothers and sisters sitting at a picnic table. The kids are with them; Alex, Christine's lad, is there, eating a custard cream. I can't see Becky; she's probably up in the Punto with the other teenagers.

'What a gordgeous mornin,' Christine says, swatting away a fly. 'Moove up there love.' Alex slides along the bench.

The group discusses the people they've spoken to; I watch the children playing by the water. One of the little lads is kicking stones with his smart leather shoes. I wonder has his mother noticed but I say nothing. Further down, a couple of the others are looking for ways to walk underneath the stone bridge.

My phone vibrates. It's a message from Siobhan:

'Evelyn left the rights of *Some Sort of Beauty* to you. Publisher wants go ahead with a new print run. What you want to do?'

I must have an odd expression because the others stop talking and look at me.

'All okhay?' Christine asks.

'Grand,' I say. I wait until they've started chatting again and I excuse myself. I walk over the damp grass, their voices receding. With each step, I find it easier to breathe.

It's strange, over the last few weeks the grief has not been what I expected. It's not something that's there all the time. In fact, there are moments when I almost forget that she's dead. Instead, my feelings come in these big waves, which feel just as bad as that first shock I got on the roof.

I'd often worried about Evelyn dying; I'd heard how she lived. Yet this was not the way I'd expected it to happen. As bad as it sounds, it was almost an anticlimax. After all she got up to, taking risks and living in that immoral way, she was simply dead because of 'time and unforeseen occurrence', like it says in Ecclesiastes. It could easily have been me, Susan or anyone else.

'You're a weak excuse for a man,' Siobhan said when I didn't go to the funeral. 'I'm embarrassed for you. Don't you have an ounce of blood in your veins, a bit of family feeling?'

Susan took the phone off me. I couldn't help my tears; after all, Evelyn was my daughter. But at the end of the day, the Bible is the Bible.

'Don't talk to your father like that,' Susan said. They fought for ages. For a man who only ever wanted a quiet life, I wondered at the circus that was going on around me.

I find a bench further along the path. Young couples have carved their initials into the wood. There's the square foil of a condom wrapper lying on the ground, another sign of the Last Days we live in.

I can hear the river further down the slope, though the branches and leaves have blocked it from view. The birds whistle. I smile. This was what Jehovah wanted, the world he created, all green and full of life.

I poke the condom wrapper with my shoe. There's a snail stuck to its underside. I remember the invite to Evelyn's first book launch coming in the post. Susan told me to ignore it and she was right, too, but Evelyn rang up anyhow. She was very abrupt, demanding that I come. I told her as clear as day that the way she and that girlfriend of hers were living was immoral.

'There's a new world coming, Dad and it's not the one you think,' she roared. 'It's not the one your fucking Bible goes on about.'

Siobhan wasn't happy either that I didn't go. 'You're a joke of a man,' she said. 'This isn't a Witness thing. It's her doing.'

I ended up buying *Some Sort of Beauty* online. There was a

strange cover photo of these feet dangling above a bed; you wouldn't know if the person was jumping, if they'd hanged themselves, or if it was some sort of religious ascension. I wasn't surprised by the picture; Evelyn always had odd taste in things. The novel had good reviews on the cover, even one from the *Sunday Independent*. But I wasn't interested in what the so-called 'critics' had to say; I just wanted to know what she'd written about, if there was anything about the Witnesses or her family.

I was surprised when I read it; there was plenty I recognised, variations on facts, but nothing bitter. There was plenty of immoral stuff in it, though; I'm glad I kept it in the shed, away from Susan. Once I'd finished, I threw it away. There was no point in dwelling on things. It was like Susan said,

'She might come back to the Truth yet. She can't be happy in that life. Deep down, she must know it's wrong.'

I glance at my watch; the others are probably waiting to get back on the ministry. Marion will have packed up, wondering where I've got to. I stand up and rub my eyes. As I walk, the bluebells touch my trousers, leaving damp streaks on the cream linen. I straighten my shirt and touch my tie knot, making sure it's in place.

I can't imagine why she'd leave her book to me. She knew my beliefs and that I didn't approve of her writing. It could only be to test me. If it just wasn't so graphic – it can hardly be 'literature' if you're writing about two girls in a bed, doing all sorts of things that you couldn't even imagine if you tried. It makes me wonder what she was doing when she was off travelling. That gay lot corrupted her; the bit with the red stiletto was outrageous altogether. Of course, she never apologised for any of it. I read her profile in *The Guardian* last year and she seemed happy with herself.

I hear some of the kids up ahead. I pause, not wanting to be with the others just yet. How did she manage to be happy? It baffles me. I couldn't picture being content without all this, without God, a bit of hope in life beyond these seventy years of struggle. I couldn't imagine being her, thinking 'this is all the life I get'. When I wake up and think about the Paradise, it keeps me sane. Looking out at the world and seeing all the injustice and suffering, I don't think I could live if I didn't know God was going to do something about it. You'd have to be heartless not to wonder, not to want things to change.

I'll have to text Siobhan and let her know the reprint won't be going ahead. I suppose she'll go off on one, calling me a doormat or something like that. She doesn't have a clue how hard it is to manage everything. All I ever wanted was a quiet life.

I touch the trunk of a sycamore. Thank goodness for nature. Nothing keeps me together like a good walk in the countryside, taking in all of God's creation. How can people believe in evolution, ignoring the beauty of it all? They must be mad.

The teens have been separated out, back into the various cars. Paul is sitting in the back seat, texting on his phone. Marion is reading a *Watchtower*.

'Did you read that lovely article on Mozambique?' she asks him. She has to repeat the question before Paul looks up from his phone.

'All okhay?' Christine asks me as I do up my seatbelt.

'No fear of me,' I say.

'I chucked away your coffee. I hoape you don't mind.'

'You're grand. Do we know where we're going?'

Paul lifts out the map. I pull out of the car park back onto the country road, slipping past hedgerows of wild onion.

'It's a pity Susan isn't well. It would've been luvely to have her out. D'you think she'd pioneer next month if I ahsked her?' Marion asks.

'Say it to her,' I reply. 'I'm sure she'd be delighted.' I pull up at the entrance to a long driveway. Between the trees, I can see a slate roof and the curving red galvanise of a barn. Christine and I step out of the car.

'I hoape there are no dogs,' she says.

'Hopefully,' I reply, frowning. Imagine, ten years and four books. Evelyn was busy all right. I read them; the last one was about Australia and the one before was about Berlin. They let me know how she lived. Of course, there was sex in them but I skipped as much as I could.

'Watch the cowpat!' Christine exclaims. In front, there's a greenish mess; its surface is cracked and flies are hovering above it. 'Are you sure you're okhay? You seem a bit distrahcted.'

'It's nothing.'

'I hoape the text wasn't bad news.'

'Not at all; it was just Siobhan. It's just the will being sorted.'

She sees that my eyes are turning glassy and touches my arm.

'You've the Paradise to look forward to.'

'I'm fine. Honestly now, I'm fine.' Her words, instead of comforting me, make me feel odd and my tears dry up. They remind me of what Susan said on the evening after Evelyn died.

'At least now she has a chance for the Paradise.'

She was right too. If Evelyn had lived, she would've been

condemned by God at the end of this system of things. But Romans says 'the wages sin pays is death'. God has forgiven her immorality – for all the things she wrote.

I lift out my phone and reply to Siobhan's message.

'Do whatever you want with the book. Just keep me out of it.'

ON EATING GRASS

Sinéad was awful jealous of me and I remember her rubbin me face into the ground and Mam wonderin what the rash was until she caught her after ages. I remember it cos Mam was tellin the nurse when she was givin Mam some exercise for her dead legs.

Like, I can't actually remember it happenin, as in, I don't remember it in me head, but it definitely happened cos Nan said I did it. That was how the week ended and wasn't I a bit exhausted and just needed me bed, so Nan said to the Guards. But sure I wasn't exhausted at all. I'd do it again, not a bother.

There was an awful lot of messin goin on since September. But it was Patrick who kicked the window and it wasn't me and I said to Teacher that I never did it and anyway it was only a tiny crack and it hadn't fallen down or nothin. Teacher didn't believe me cos she'd sent me home before cos I wouldn't take off me jersey. She said she didn't give two hoots about football and I said we'd been in the quarter finals and it was soccer anyway and if she didn't like it she could feck off home to England.

Teacher took us to Dublin to the Natural Gallery cos she said it's the best art in Ireland and some of it was good but I didn't like it, just borin pictures of Our Lord lookin sick like the ones in Nan's house. Sure wasn't he always dyin. But half of it was shite anyway cos I coulda done better. This one fella with a mad German name or somethin did this picture of these boats sailin and it was like somethin a baby coulda done. Patrick was laughin at this one of a woman's arse hangin out, it was feckin huge and we were laughin and makin farts and Teacher told us to shut up or we'd have to go sit on the bus even though everyone else was laughin too. We were lookin at them for ages and me legs were gettin tired so I had to keep swappin them over but we got Taytos and coke and then we went to the shop with books and toppers of Our Lord lookin green. Me and Patrick found this book with photos of women with tits and Patrick drew moustaches but I said nothin and we went home.

Me and Patrick took a can from Da's boot on Monday cos it was lyin there and we went behind Nan's shed and drank it. I only drank some cos Patrick did and he called me chicken so I drank half of it and he said I felt sick and I said I didn't even though I did. And I said to him if he was such a hard man why didn't he feckin drink the rest of it and stop talkin shite. I kept burpin and Patrick said I couldn't burp the alphabet so I did and got sick and then the dog started lickin it and it was cool but I thought it was disgustin.

Mary Roberson's been on the telly the whole time wantin to be president n'all and Da thinks she'll get it cos any old eejit could do that job. She looks nice but he said don't they all look nice until they're elected and then they turn into a right shower of bastards.

Sinéad got the attic cos she was older and Mam said she couldn't be trustin me with the steps as I was always hurtin meself but I said to her I was grand and wasn't I always climbin things. And she said what was wrong with me own room but I said it was unfair cos Sinéad got a lock on hers and I'd none on mine. Mam said when I was in Secondary I could have one and she said I smelt funny and had I been sick and I got an awful fright cos of the can.

Sure wasn't Da a right bastard on Tuesday when he found out that I'd taken his can. I know Mam hates him too cos I saw her lookin all sick when he went to kiss her. I wish he'd feck off back to the army and leave us alone. The bruises on me legs were awful sore. When he stuck the pipe back on the hoover I said it to him 'you're a right cunt' and sure that only made him worse. I thought I'd never get me breath but I didn't cry. I was lookin at him the whole time. And no dinner either and I was feckin starvin. He said somethin and I told him to feck off with his Bible. I showed them bruises to Patrick and Patrick said I should tell Teacher but they'd only take me off and sure who'd look after Mam. Sinéad's only a girl, like. She always cryin at everythin.

Patrick said I was chicken and I said to him I wasn't and I wasn't either. I didn't cos Mam said to me I wasn't to fight. And Mam is in a wheelchair and she's enough to be worryin about except me scrappin in fights and she's in pain too. She doesn't like me with bruises cos they remind her of Our Lord dyin, that's what Nan said, but I said to her Our Lord died for sins so I better make a few or else he needn't have been dyin at all.

Nan didn't like that but that's only cos she loves Our Lord and there's a picture of him with his heart floatin out in front of him and he looks awful sick but that's cos his heart's floatin outside of him. I asked Nan how could he be livin without his heart inside him and she said it's the holy ghost which is a third of God's glory. And I asked her what it's like and she said it's electricity. And I felt awful bad cos I was watchin telly and usin up God's glory when poor baby Jesus needed it.

Mam wanted a girl, that's what Sinéad says when she gets

all snotty and tells me to fuck off out of her room. But she was only a baby anyway so how would she know and Mam hardly wanted two girls cos wasn't one bad enough, and I should know cos she's my sister and she's a right aul bitch – that's what Patrick said to me when she told him he had to go home cos his Mam had rang and she hadn't.

Mam hasn't been herself for a long time. She gets desperate sad since the accident when her legs stopped workin. She has them n all, but they don't move cos she hurt her back and her brain messages don't work. She used to have a push chair but then they nagged them at the hospital for ages and they gave her this electric one which I rode but Sinéad whacked me on the head and said if I broke it she'd wake Mam.

Teacher was nice to me when she heard me Mam was in a chair but I said at least she wasn't dead, sure wouldn't that be worse, but Teacher tapped me head and I felt all hot but I didn't say anything. I felt bad then cos I wasn't laughin at Mam, just I didn't want her bein all sorry for me, like, or for Mam, even though she'd be cryin sometimes.

Patrick looks at Mam sometimes and I give him a dig. He calls her and Da Mr and Mrs Murphy, suckin up like, and I told him to not bother cos he sounds like a right eejit and no one calls them that. He picked flowers for Mam once too and I heard Uncle Jim say to Aunty Catherine that it was a shame that Mam was like that cos she was so pretty.

Sure didn't Da say that he wanted to teach me a lesson last Thursday, sayin I couldn't leave the table till I'd eaten me dinner. Me legs got fierce tired after a while from standin but he said that'd make me eat a lot quicker. But I wasn't goin to eat nothin and then him sayin he'd break the stubbornness out of me and I was lookin at him straight and the cabbage went all wet.

Sure when he finished I was still there. In the end he put me in the cupboard and said I couldn't come out till I was done. I put the cabbage in the coat pockets but it wouldn't all fit and it was fallin out everywhere. And then Da got the pipe and that was the end of it. He said somethin about Jesus and starvin black babies but sure me legs were stingin so I could hardly take any notice of him.

I heard the nurse talkin to Nan on Friday and she was sayin stuff that got me awful hot. Nan was sayin it was the guilt that turned Da sour and wouldn't Mam be up and about if he hadn't been in the car all steamed up. And him with cans in the boot. I was mad with temper after that. I hated him, so I did, and wanted to hit him a belt and I said it to Patrick that I did, but Da's bigger.

Then on Sunday, sure I was down by the gate and didn't he come out at me all swingin and shoutin, holdin that coat with the cabbage fallin out everywhere. I never seen him as hot in the face, steamin he was. He wasn't lookin where he was goin at all, just swingin and roarin, and didn't he trip over and get a mouthful of grass.

I got close and there was a shockin smell of drink off him. I was awful hot thinkin of Mam, not scared or nothin. I thought I'd leave him there, but then sure he'd only wake up and be annoyin us all. And sure wasn't there a rock in the flowers and I thought I'd hit him a clatter with it while I'd the chance. So I did anyhow. I hit him a mighty whack on the head and that shut him up good.

I don't remember smackin him a few times but I musta cos Nan said I did. I don't remember kickin him either. I wanted to come home but they wouldn't leave me, even though Teacher'd be wonderin where I was.

Nan told me Da was dead but sure I never asked cos I didn't care. She was mad blessin herself and sayin I should be speakin to the Priest. But she never liked Da anyway and sure at least now he'll leave poor Mam alone. Didn't I say to Nan, aren't we all grand enough without havin him around the place, actin the hard fella?

She didn't like that so I promised that I'd behave for Mam and even for Teacher when I was back at school and that I wouldn't be messin with Patrick. But Nan just kept shakin her head and fiddlin with her rosary. She kept on sayin again and again, 'sure we'll see what'll happen... sure we'll see...'

DABDA

Where do I sit now? That chair, is it? D'you always sit by the door? I suppose you never know what sort of whackjob is going to walk in next. You don't have a spare cushion, do you? It's my knee; it's still banjaxed since the accident. Have you read all of those? My God, I don't know how people have the time; I'd never have the patience.

I know, I know. I meant to come but between one thing and another, with work and then Pat was sick, I couldn't get away at all. Your man must be mad sending me here. I was laughing to Pat, saying I'd rather be sent down. Nothing personal like, but these sorts of things, you'd have to be going a bit soft to be coming to them. I'd rather just be getting on with it, not mamby-bambying about, no offence, like.

I don't know, sure. I'll have to stick the twelve weeks anyhow, get the form and have this mess sorted out. I've never had anything like this before. He was very harsh with the sentence; the solicitor couldn't believe it. It's better than AA, I suppose. I couldn't hack that pack of moaning Michaels. How long have you been doing this? We can have a grand couple of chats. I'll bring biscuits next time. A fine job you have, being paid to gossip. I'm only joking, of course; I'm sure you do great things.

What do you do with them anyhow? It's all talking about their past, moaning about their mammies. Don't get me wrong, when you hear what some go through, it'd make you shudder. But didn't we all go through something or other growing up. You've just gotta mind yourself and keep your neck above water.

My clan? I'm married to Pat seven years. We're very happy, so no need to go rooting there. I've the two lads from my first marriage all right. Let me think now, Kevin must be twenty-five and Laura is ten months younger. They both finished university last year. Mad studying they were, though Laura is the brains of the operation.

He studied English – was it English? I forget. It was some arty thing anyhow. He was always a dreamer but he seems to be doing grand. Ah, what Mammy gets to see enough of her kids? You've to let them off into the world and not run around after them.

Laura is very pretty all right; she takes after her Mammy. She's her father's nose but that can't be helped. Still, he was a looker himself back in the day. No, I haven't seen him since Kevin's wedding. But is there any such thing as a good end to a marriage? The merry widow, me arse.

So what are we going to talk about? You probably have a bunch of leaflets to hand me on drink, and I don't even drink above twice a year. It's madness that they've me hauled in here when there are winos on the street glued to their bottles of Scrumpy Jack. Well, I know that, of course. But in all fairness, it's a waste of money. As usual, it's taxpayers' cash down the swanee.

That night? Pat was driving. I'd a glass of wine with my dinner but nothing more than anybody else would have of a weekend. My sister was down in Costigan's and we were meeting her about nine. We've always been very close. She's mad out; if there was someone who could do with a bit of therapy, it'd be herself. She's a lunatic. Honestly, she sent her Jimmy running up the road one night, lobbing the kitchen knives after him.

Christ, I know I shouldn't be laughing but I have this image of them. Of course, she shouldn't be drinking at all with those tablets she's on. Still, she needs to blow off a bit of steam; she's two young fellas under the age of fifteen. You should see the grand set of legs she has. Don't I have them myself, whatever about my belly – don't get me started on that thing! Honestly, not a bite passes my lips after my breakfast until dinner time and I still can't shift the weight. I've warned Laura about it, telling her if she doesn't watch herself that flat stomach of hers will soon vanish.

Jesus, I'm after waffling on a bit. I'm always mad for the chats, an aul gossip with the girls in the salon. Pat is the complete opposite, would you believe; he never says a word. But don't opposites attract. He's very like the children's father in a way, both electricians, but Pat's no temper at all. By God, that other fella; we'd some rows. I'd to take the lads to that battered women's place once when they were wee babbies. Honestly, the life I've had! You wouldn't believe it if you read it in a book.

He did rear them. It didn't go to court or anything because I didn't want the lads to be mixed up in all that custody stuff. They were only two or three at the time. Well anyhow, that's another tale for you. My God, you're a terror for writing stuff down. No one else will be reading that? Can I take a look? Well, I'd rather you didn't write down that sort of thing. I mean it's hardly the point.

I know, I'm a terror for wandering off. Anyhow, we went for a couple in Costigan's with Tracey. She's not able for the drink, though; it goes one way or the other: either she's the life and soul or she's picking a fight. Didn't I one time have to tell her to pull up her knickers when she was about to take a slash in the beer garden. Thank God the bouncers didn't see;

we'd have been kicked out. We got kicked out enough times from Kiely's growing up, but nearly everyone did back then. It was outside Kiely's that I met the children's father, would you believe. I gave him a shift; Jesus, can you believe we used to call it that. Ah, look, there you go with the biro again. I can't say anything to you. Why don't you tell me something? Nothing like that happen to yourself? It can't be me doing all the work.

Really? Never? My God, I couldn't be like that. You've got to live after all. Now, where are you from originally? Ah, very nice. I've a cousin down that direction. Have you been to that restaurant there, down on the water? Yes, Jacob's; it's gorgeous. Pat and I stayed in the B&B next door and had a fabulous dinner there. We headed for a few scoops in O'Donnell's after. Are you down that direction any more? Ah, sure at least it's close enough for a weekend visit.

Tracey got in an awful state that night. She must've had a few before she came out, more than my glass of wine anyhow. She was probably tipping away all afternoon and God knows with her medicine mixed in as well. It wasn't even half nine and Pat and I had to drag her home. It was just as well the kids were with their father. Ah yeah, he survived the knife throwing all right; it was nothing but the grace of God that she missed him. It's very sad, really. Where she lives wouldn't be the best spot either; that estate is as rough as they come. Pat and I built this gorgeous place outside of town; he was able to build most of it himself, so we aren't saddled with a mortgage like the rest of Ireland.

Do they come to see me? When they can they do but it isn't easy with them both working in the city. Things have always been very hard to arrange with their father; he's always kicking up a stink. He's a right bastard, excuse my language, but if I start on about him I'll never shut up. So much for an hour, we'll be here till Sunday.

What time are we at now? Thirty minutes to go. Twenty? Of course, I forget about these fifty-minute hours. We all come in and get our fifty-minute 'shot' to keep us going for the week. Have you really read all those books or are they just for show? I suppose most of them are from college. What about those chairs you see in films with people lying on them? I was disappointed not to see one when I walked in. chayz longs – that's them. Pat got me one for the bedroom; he said he'd feed me grapes off it but it's only collecting dust, of course. What's that book about? You don't mind?

DABDA – what does it mean? Five stages, really? DABDA, DABDA, abracadabra! The way it's written! If it was that easy, wouldn't we all be cured? I mean, Tracey's been to as many therapists as you can think of, but they did her no favours. She's still on as many yokes as ever. You can't talk some things out; she'd an awful time growing up. My God, some of the things that happened.

That night? You saw the report? I didn't think they gave out those sorts of things. It's a bit much, isn't it? I mean, with privacy laws and that EU crack. In all fairness, I don't think that's on at all. Can I complain to someone about that? The judge? I suppose it's too late now anyhow.

The wedding – that wasn't great now. Sure, you've read the file, though I'd say that thing is about as near to reality as Coronation Street. Ridiculous really, the stuff that was said in court; they were making out I was a right, well, I can't even think of the word. I'm very surprised they'd give out information like that. I mean, I haven't even seen it. You can hardly blame me for what happened. It wasn't like anyone got hurt anyhow; a tree and a bumper – I'm hardly a murderer.

Can you imagine not getting an invite to your own son's wedding? I know I wasn't around when they were young when I was setting up with Pat. But we had to go to England. It was the eighties for Christ's sake; we hadn't two pennies to rub together. When I had Kevin, his father and I were in a mobile home, waiting on a council house. Nineteen with a baby and living in a mobile home, and wasn't their father out most of the time on his motorbike with the gang. You can't blame me for needing to get out. But the lads got the wrong idea altogether, thinking that I didn't care because I'd let them stay with their daddy. They didn't remember what he was like back then. Didn't I have to go to that battered women's place.

No, I'd never have left them be fostered. The courts never know what they're doing; they're a right pack of eejits.

Have you been listening to me at all? I had to go to England with Pat. We didn't have a penny in the bank and I couldn't live near that fella. The lads were fine, of course; he only had a temper towards me. He hated me and didn't he do everything he could to poison them against me. I tried to meet them a couple of times along the way but he was having none of it. It wasn't till I moved back here with Pat that I was able to see them.

Would you mind if I got myself a glass of water from the machine? Pity there's not a drop of vodka in it. He'd drive ya to drink, that man. Will I get you one? No? I suppose you're used to people rattling on about one thing or another. Don't we all have a story at the end of the day? The problem is, of course, it's the stories that people don't talk about that are the interesting ones.

It was actually Laura who contacted me first. She'd started college and had moved out of home, so she could give me a call without him kicking off. She told Kevin, too; he wasn't so keen now. I don't think he wanted to come. We'd a coffee in Scott's; they were all grown up anyhow. He was the head off his father with that black hair and eyes, but she was the image of meself. We could've been sisters, the same long legs. The only thing is my belly; after I had them two, there was no keeping it in shape. Honestly, not a bite passes my lips after my toast in the morning until I'd have the dinner made for Pat and I still can't shift the weight. Poor aul Laura, she'll have the same problem in a few years I'd say. Kevin will be grand but he'll probably go as bald as his father.

We met up a couple of times. It wasn't great, really. I was forever buying them bits and pieces and giving them a few bob so I don't know what the problem was. Their father didn't help, of course. He was on and on at them. Let me tell you, I told them a few home truths about that man. They didn't know any of it, of course. What he'd said about me, I couldn't even repeat. The lies, they were un-be-lieve-able. He'd said that I was the one clawing at him back then. Sure, look at the size of me; I'm as weak as water.

Anyhow, Laura stayed a few times at the house and we were getting on great. She was fairly troubled though. I knew she was drinking along with plenty of other stuff. You should've seen her; she was as thin as a rake. I had it out with her in the end. She said I was jealous and I could, y'know, fuck off. The brother took her side, of course and that was the end of that.

Can you imagine, she thought I was jealous. As if a woman would be jealous of her own daughter! Look at me anyway; what do I have to be jealous of? I've a great life with Pat and look at this set of legs, no one can ever believe my age when I tell them. Jealous of her! My God, she'd say anything before admit she was as messed up as her father. Kevin's no better, mind, as hard as marble.

It was at Kevin's wedding that they all kicked off at me. I still can't believe I didn't get an invite; I only heard about it from a cousin. I sent Kevin a message, asking him straight out about the whole thing. He didn't even have the decency to get back to me.

Exactly, that's what happened. I didn't bother with the church, as his father's lot were there. But I had a present for Kevin and his wife and I wanted a picture for the house. Of course, we'd met up with Tracey at Costigan's and she was as pissed as a fart. I'd a couple of drinks myself, would you blame me, like? Me stuck in a pub, while my son was getting married up the street.

So anyhow, after we'd got Tracey home, I said to Pat that I was going to get a photo at least and drop off the present. In all fairness to him, Pat said not to bother because there'd be all sorts of trouble. I wasn't having any of it. I'd had three Coronas but I knew myself well enough. I was well within my rights.

Pat dropped me over and wasn't there a big scene with their arsehole father. I can't believe I used to be married to that man. The second he saw me, him and that new wife of his, he went for me like I'd a shotgun pointed at the room. He was an embarrassment. The look on Laura's face; she didn't know what to make of it. Would you believe it though, Kevin was glaring at me, though it was his father who was doing all the roaring. I said to Kevin, are you going to let your father speak to me like that? But he said nothing. Laura was no better.

Thank God Pat was there, that's all I can say. If he hadn't pulled me off, I'd have went for that fucker. Of course, poor old Pat got the brunt of it in the hallway. I never saw red like it. I stormed off anyhow; I thought a drive might cool me down but, sure, y'know the rest. I got distracted and the car ended up against that tree.

So you see, it wasn't the drink at all. It was the shock of it. Could you blame me? That langer roaring at me like it was nineteen-eighty-three. It's a God-awful shame, let me tell you, what he's done to those kids. I remember thinking it was the last time I'd have anything to do with them. But y'know what it's like to be a mother; I'll always be here for them.

Christ, it must be fifty minutes at this point. Y'know when you start talking, it's mad how you can go off. You'd think I was making it up. Isn't it warm in here? Can I open the window a crack?

Three minutes? I'd say you nearly have enough. You won't be needing me to come back after all that. You think? I mean, it was hardly my fault. He was a charmer, he always was. Sure, I had to leave, what else could I do?

BRUSH AND GUT

I might go back to bed for an hour once I've made breakfast for the two of them. They'd be lost without me, the young fella needing help with his sandwiches and the older one wanting his coffee and porridge.

You've probably heard of my husband Gearóid de Barra, or at least his paintings. Mary Robinson bought one once. These days he's massive in the States, people wanting his sea pictures in their hallways. That's why he changed his name to Irish a few years back. He didn't think Gerry Barry had the same ring across the pond. I told him I didn't think it would matter as he was 'the Irish Turner' – at least that's what they wrote in *Circa*. I've a copy of it in a drawer upstairs along with all the other clippings.

A man like Ger needs his breakfast. Between his boat and the painting, he's always busy. But I knew it'd be the case when I married him. You marry a great man and you've to share him with the world – sure look at politicians' wives. Now those women have it tough. At least I've Ger's paintings around the house when he isn't about.

I'll have to wake the two of them once the kettle boils. I wonder could I have a smoke out the window before they come downstairs, though it gets in my clothes and I've told Ger that I quit. But that was before Lorcan was born. Ger must've copped on by now that I still like the odd one.

I open the window. The daffodils are out and I get an idea which I write on the back of a receipt. I love getting inspiration like that, just out of the blue. I probably won't go back to bed after all as my group is at eleven. The coffee smells delicious. What drives me mad is I'd love to write how coffee smells but it's one of those sorts of things that can only be described as itself. Comparing it to something else doesn't work at all.

I poke the chicken I got out of the freezer last night. It's nearly defrosted. I tip the watery blood off the plate and down the sink. For such a manly man, Ger doesn't like gore at all; I always gut the fish he brings home from the boat. Though a few years back he did a couple of paintings of mackerel up close; they were as real looking as photographs, their sinews and everything. They'll never sell, I told him, who'd want to have them above their fireplace? Of course I was right. I've the practical head of the two of us. But I didn't want to hurt his feelings so I hung them up in the kitchen around the corner from where people eat, just above the bins.

I glance at them, the cloudy eyes on the mackerel. What can he have been thinking? I suppose in about fifty years, after he's dead, half of Ireland will be wanting them; that's the way it goes in these arty circles.

His porridge is done and I take it off the heat. I lift a bowl out of the cupboard. We've lovely china; I'm glad Ger put his foot down when we first moved in. We'd a few quid from my parents and we could've kitted the place out a couple of times over with stuff from Argos. But he wouldn't hear of it; he'd only buy the best. We bought these expensive sheets, hundreds they were, and didn't have enough even for a kettle. For a year, I'd to boil water in a saucepan. But gradually we bought more good stuff and now the house is a piece of art in itself. I always get people commenting on the oak dresser and chrome Aga in the kitchen.

I look at the clock. It's been three minutes since I poured

the water into the coffee pot. I'd better wake them up. It's almost eight o'clock and Lorcan needs to be out the door by half past. I hope he's got himself up and dressed at least; he's a terror for falling back to sleep – you'd think he was eighteen, not eight.

'Would you like a drop more?' I say to Ger as he finishes his coffee. His hair is wet and he's in his dressing gown, that Ralph Lauren one I got him for Christmas. He picked it out before I bought it. I've learnt over the years not to buy him anything without getting the thumbs up; he's peculiar about his appearance. When we were first seeing each other, he'd always say he loved the jumpers and pants I got for him but he never wore them. Honestly, I was never as bad as him about clothes. A nice top and jeans did me grand at college; I'd my figure then from all the rowing. Now, I'm forever looking for tops with a nice loose waist. After a child, it's impossible to keep your figure.

The hair on his chest is peeping through his robe. He's a very sexy man, even now he's forty. Even in a room full of young fellas, he can still cut a fine figure. When he was younger, I remember he'd be the only thing in the room that any of us girls would be looking at; his paintings on the walls hardly seemed to matter. I was pretty enough all right, but nothing to that. Those dark eyes and sallow skin – you'd think he was descended from pirates.

'I'm okay, Ange. You haven't seen my keys lying about anywhere?' he asks.

'They're in the hall drawer,' I say. 'Honestly, if your head wasn't screwed on.' He smiles at me. Sometimes I think I must be boring for him; I know I'm no great wit. Half the time when I'm at these fancy events with him I don't know what the hell people are saying.

It seems that Ger can read my thoughts; he pulls me close so that my thighs touch off the kitchen table. His hand slips around my backside, grabbing it. I enjoy the feel of his palm, though my backside's a lot fatter than it used to be. Lorcan looks up at us. He has the same eyes as his father. I'm glad he takes after him; he'll be breaking girls' hearts one day. At least for now he's still my boy.

'Do you want any more cornflakes?' I ask him. He nods. I know what he's like; he could eat a boxful. Boys his age are like bottomless pits for food. I glance at the clock; he'll never be out the door for half past if he continues making his cornflake moats in the breakfast bowl, trying to keep the sugary ones from falling into the milk. I try to hurry him on but he can never leave a cornflake in the bowl.

'Can I have some money for the shop?' Lorcan asks his father as I wash his bowl. He wouldn't ask me, of course, knowing I'd probably only give him a euro.

'Take a look in the jar there,' Ger replies. On the bookshelf, there's a glass where he throws the change out of his wallet every now and again. I keep saying I'll count it; there must be fifty quid there at least. Lorcan lifts out a number of coins, ignoring the bronze ones.

'Don't be eating too much rubbish now. I've made you lunch,' I say, spying him from the sink, my marigolds lifted up so the water doesn't drip everywhere. But it's too late; Lorcan has pocketed the money in his school pants and is making for the staircase. I sigh, turning to Ger. 'So what are you at for the day?'

'I'll head down to the gallery to Gráinne, check those shipments and crack on with the commission.'

'The one of the dolphins? The sketches are lovely for it.'

'They're seals.'

I laugh. I can see he's annoyed but he takes no notice of me really.

'Ah, you know what I'm like. A seal or a dolphin, they're all one and the same to me. Will you be back for your supper?'

'I'm not sure yet. I might head out on the boat for a while.' I can tell he's sulking. That's his artistic temperament; he'll get over himself in a minute.

'Try not to be too late. Lorcan and I never get to see you these days.'

He doesn't reply and rewraps his dressing gown instead, hiding his chest.

'I'm gonna get dressed; it's getting late. I'll drop Lorcan off.'

'Would you ever pick me up some milk on the way back? And some Oxo cubes?' I'll need them for the chicken gravy.

'Make a list.'

'Don't take too long. Lorcan has to be gone in ten minutes.' I know what Ger is like. Some mornings he'd be preening himself for a good half hour in front of the mirror, even after he's had a shower. He's worse than a girl really; I've told him as much enough times. But I'm secretly glad; I could have one of those awful dirty husbands who stinks of sweat and farts. I clear his bits off the table, knowing ten minutes will pass and I'll be shouting up the stairs, telling them to hurry up.

They're both gone. It's nearly nine o'clock and I'm just out of the shower. I'll have to get ready if I'm to get to McCurtain Street for eleven. It's my turn to bring in cakes; I'll pick up something from that bakery around the corner. One of the great things about living in Kinsale is all the lovely shops you discover: little boutiques, jewellers and bakeries hidden down the old laneways. There are some gorgeous fishmongers down by the docks with fish fresh from the boats, though I rarely have to go buy any as Ger catches a hell of a lot. We were lucky we bought this house when we did, before the prices started to skyrocket. I'd say we'd nearly get double for it these days compared to what we paid in the nineties.

I dry my hair and wonder should I give Mam a ring. I know she's been worried about Daddy since he had the heart attack. He's talking about going back to work but I don't know how he'll manage the lectures at all. That Italian professor, what's his name, Fabrini or flannel-something, is running the department for him; I know Daddy's worried that your man will end up having the job permanently. It's hard for Daddy to be moping about the house after being the man he was. Sure wasn't it he who put Ger on the map, writing him that review in *The Irish Times*.

Jesus, they were the days, all that excitement. I still can't believe Ger took a blind bit of notice of me. When I think of him in those lovely crisp white shirts and smelling of some sort of aftershave; I was weak for him, as were all the girls. He'd an eye for them, too but for some reason or other he settled on myself.

I sit down in front of the mirror and spray my hair so that it stays in place. There are a few lines around my eyes – all part of getting older. I put on a bit of foundation, which Ger thinks is too dark for my skin but it puts a bit of colour in my cheeks anyhow. I add a touch of mascara and lip gloss; I know these poetic types don't like anything too glamorous.

It's my clothes that bother me most of all. I'd love to get my figure back. Before, I used to dream that Ger would paint me naked, just like your one from Titanic, but now I don't like taking my clothes off in front of him. It's my stomach that gets me; it's all white and flabby.

I pick out some jeans and a black top, as black is nice and slimming. As I put on my bra, I hear the front door open and the rustling of bags.

'Your stuff's on the kitchen table,' Ger roars up. 'I'll see you later.'

'Would you ever...' I call out. The front door has already closed.

There are eight of us altogether and the apple tart and banoffi are being demolished. I try to just have a bit of the apple tart, as I don't want to put on any more pounds. But the woman in that bakery is a genius; I tell her every time I go in. In the end, I decide to have a bit of banoffi too.

It must be great to have a talent. I do throw down a few lines for this poetry thing and the girls are very nice but I know I'm no Seamus Heaney or Eavan Boland. Sometimes I wonder is it because I'm happy that I can't write the kind of poems I'd like to; I think I might be too content to write about famine roads or, you know, sexual difficulties. It seems dissatisfaction is one of the things you need to be a good artist. Sure, looking at this group, there's Shirley with poems about her divorce, Marie with the cancer she had, and Caroline who lost her nephew all those years back. They all have important things to say, unlike me. Half the time I'm writing about spring, love or daffodils – silly stuff like that.

There's something I'm missing compared to these types of people. Even growing up, at those dinners we'd be invited to with all sorts of intellectuals and artists who were visiting UCC, the language they all spoke was not the way I spoke, or what your average Joe Soap might come out with. Artists are like a different race from the rest of us.

Look at Ger; he decided to change his name, just like that. I'd never have had the nerve. Or sometimes he gets up in the middle of the night and goes down to the studio painting or out on the boat thinking. I ask what he'd be thinking and he just shrugs.

I guess we two races each have our place; my type is as important as theirs, really. As I always say, the artist may be the one on display, the cake so to speak, but where would the cake be without the cake tin that supported it? Who'd collect Lorcan from school and have a proper dinner ready? Ger would be half-starved if it wasn't for me. When we first started dating, I remember being shocked when I stayed over at his place after being used to my home. There was barely a tin of beans in the cupboards and a draught blowing around the sashes. The only thing right about the place was his wardrobe of ironed shirts and polished shoes.

Marie touches my hand; it's my turn to read my poetry. The seven women are looking and I know my new poem is nowhere near as interesting as the ones that have gone before me. It's a love poem, which makes me feel a bit exposed. I make a joke about the cakes, how I can barely read I'm so stuffed. The women smile and I feel less nervous. I hope it isn't too mushy. I know they hate when I go sentimental.

The girls are very nice to me when I finish. I know it's not really to their taste, far too light for them to really get their teeth into. The ending of it I'm not sure about either; over the past month it's been bugging me, especially when I'm about to drop off. A lot of the words I got from the thesaurus. I only got a second class honours in my degree, and a low one at that.

Caroline asks me have I shown the poem to Ger. They

know I'm married to a great painter and are always interested to hear a story or two. It's probably the reason they allow me to keep meeting them. It can hardly be my poetry anyhow. The meeting runs overtime by about an hour. Three of us have to leave to go pick up children. I hope Lorcan won't be too annoyed that I'm late but at least he has his Gameboy that he can be messing around on. I'm sure there'll be one or two other boys about for him to kick a football with. Yet he's like his father, not great with team sports.

I drive Lorcan home and my nerves settle; perhaps my poem isn't so bad. It has that poet-y sound about it, not too overblown like some of my early stuff. Promising, that's what Caroline said. I could enter it somewhere but I'd rather leave it in a cupboard for now and wait for 'promising' to become something else.

The sun is low in the sky; the narrow street on which we live is already in shadow. It's been a bright March day but when the evening sets in, it gets cold fast. I fiddle with the keys, dropping my shopping on the pavement, along with the bunch of tulips I treated myself to from Tesco.

I check the phone in the hall for messages. There's no word from Ger. I hear the television being switched on in the sitting room and I tell Lorcan to turn it off till he's finished his homework. But I can still hear the sound of Pokemon. I call Ger; the phone rings six times. He never answers, but generally will ring me back at some point. I wonder how the seals, or was it dolphins, are coming on. There'll be a massive cheque when that comes through. We might even get a trip to New York out of it.

I turn on the kitchen light, placing the tulips on the counter. They're still in their buds. 'Origin – Amsterdam, Holland' is on the label. I smile; surely it's not that hard to source Irish tulips in spring. I fill a large square glass with water and add the free sachet of plant food. Lining up the tulips, I cut four inches off the stems, before standing them upright and tapping them on the cutting board, checking their length.

I place them in the vase; the heads barely come over the top. It's a trick I learnt from my mother; in about three days, the tulips will have grown with lovely straight stems. If I'd left them as they were, they'd droop over the sides. I throw the ends in the bin on top of the plastic wrapping. I glance at Ger's paintings of the gutted fishes, those ugly scummy eyes and realise being practical has its advantages. Sometimes you have to be tough on things, how else will they ever be beautiful?

The television is on; I shout with a tone that Lorcan cannot ignore. The noise stops and Lorcan comes into the kitchen and drops his rucksack onto a chair. This is a ritual of ours; I prepare the dinner while Lorcan finishes his homework at the table.

'Did Miss O'Connor give you lots to do?' I ask.

'Not much.' I know he wants to convince me of this so he can finish quickly and return to the living room.

'Don't take that out,' I say, glancing at his Gameboy, which he's put beside his maths book. He slides it about four inches along the table. I turn back to the worktop and begin preparing the chicken. I tear open the plastic bag it's in. There's more juice, streaks of clotted blood amongst the water. I rinse the skin under the tap, clearing away all the fluid. I'm careful as I cut off some excess skin with one of the steel knives from the block; those knives would cut through bone as if it was butter.

After a few minutes, I ask Lorcan if he needs a hand with

anything but he says he's all right. He's a smart child, taking after his father, all intelligence and no practicality. The phone rings as I put the potatoes on to boil, softening them ready for roasting. It's Ger.

'How's the painting going?' I ask.

'Grand. I'm still planning it out.'

'It'll be great.'

'Listen, I won't make it home for dinner at all. I'm gonna stick with this for a bit longer.'

'But I've the dinner in the oven.'

'I'll heat it up when I get in.'

'You wouldn't be half an hour getting there and back.'

'You don't understand Ange. When I'm in a flow, I've got to stick with it.' There's no answer I can give to this. After all, his art is our bread and butter.

'Well look, try not to be too late. Poor Lorcan is missing his daddy.' I rub Lorcan's head. He's chewing the end of his pencil, staring at his times tables.

'I'll see you later, right?' Ger says.

'Sure.'

'Love you,' he says to me. It's something he's got into the habit of saying recently when he knows I'm annoyed.

'Okay, bye...' I relent at the last second. 'Me too, love you.'

I park the Land Rover on the slope that leads up to Spanish Point. It's my favourite spot in Kinsale, the fortress at the entrance to the bay. The sun is low on the horizon; Lorcan hops out and kicks stones as he walks with me towards the entrance. I tell him to do up his coat, the wind is cold.

I'm glad to see the entrance is open. I used to run over to the fort a couple of times a week when we first moved here, before I got pregnant. I think maybe I'll start running again.

Ger messaged to say he was hopping on the boat, that he needs an hour to clear his head after the day painting. I tried to call him back but he didn't answer.

It's almost seven o'clock; I wonder if we're all right, though I guess he has done this sort of thing before. He's a solitary spirit. But we definitely don't sleep together as much as we used to; probably because he's tired with all his work. I wonder if I should get more involved with the gallery, though I know he has Gráinne managing that and doesn't like me to interfere.

Lorcan isn't happy I've taken him out for a walk, away from the television. It can't be good for him. He gets so transfixed you have to stand in between him and it to get a response. I can see the Gameboy is sticking out of his pocket even though I told him to leave it at home. Maybe we should get him a dog, so he doesn't become a complete recluse. What'll he be like when he's a teen? I'd be worried he'd be bored of the dog after a week and I'd spend the next fifteen years cleaning up after it.

We walk along the ramparts; it's a massive fortress, ruined of course but the ruins are well preserved. It's lovely to look out over the harbour from this height. The water is calm, the colour of the setting sun. A few boats are out. It's a wonder Ger doesn't get lost in all that; he can barely locate his wallet half the time.

There are a couple of boats sailing by the far pier casting long reflections on the water. One of them is small; maybe it's the Island Time. I wonder if he's caught any fish. They might be nice with some white sauce and mashed potatoes tomorrow.

'Mam, I'm freezing,' says Lorcan.

I nod. The sun is pretty much gone.

'Sorry, darling. We'll head back now,' I reply, squeezing his shoulder. I find myself slightly tearful and I'm not sure why. Perhaps it's just the wind; it's hard being married to an artist, always having the smaller share of their attention.

'Do you mind if we pass by the gallery a second?' I say to Lorcan. 'I'll only be five minutes.' I'm curious to see how Ger's painting is coming on. At least he's out of the gallery and won't be fussing as he usually does when I come to see his work, over-explaining it all.

'Can I have some Rice Krispies when we get home?' Lorcan asks.

'Of course you can.' I drive along the coastline, slipping into the narrow streets of the town. It's hard to find parking and I'm forced to stop at the far end of the street. I can see the red gallery front in the distance. It's a beautiful building that we have: all modern but at the same time we kept the exposed bricks inside. It was all Ger's idea, of course.

Lorcan stays in the car on his Gameboy. I walk up the cobbled path, past the miniature gift shops and boutiques to the gallery. I lift out my keys to put in the gallery door but I can see at the back Ger and Gráinne are talking. She's smiling and slapping his chest. He's dressed in his crisp white shirt and perfectly creased Hugo Boss trousers.

I step back from the door, feeling a little dizzy. I turn and walk back to the Jeep, as I don't want Lorcan to come looking for me. I don't want him asking why his father is not on the boat, bringing fish home for tomorrow's dinner.

I clean away the dinner things. The antique grandfather clock in the hallway rang ten a short while ago. I don't feel different from usual, just a slight dizziness that I cannot shake. It's not like the first time this happened when I was crying all the time. I think I understand things – him – a bit better.

I'm not sure what I'll do so I think I'll wait for him to come home and see what happens. I should be angry, wondering why he'd be like this when I've only ever supported him with everything he wants to do. I know I'm not as pretty as I once was. Then again, I still had my figure when he first did it, so it can't be my looks.

I guess he's always being tempted, being the handsome man he is. There's a danger if a man is too handsome he'll always have offers and he might slip up from time to time. Can I forgive him? After all, he is who he is. Nearly all of them throughout history did it; I mean, look at Picasso. It's as I thought: artists need to be dissatisfied and, if that's the case, it's inevitable that these things will happen.

The front door opens. I feel myself tense. I can hear the rustling of plastic bags.

'Hello,' he says. He sounds happy. I don't turn around. I'm not sure I can speak and not give myself away.

'Hi.' I dab my nose with the back of my rubber gloves.

'I caught some mackerel,' he says, dropping the bag onto the counter.

'What was it like out?'

'Ah, good. The sun was beautiful on the water.'

'Did you clear your head?' I continue scrubbing the roasting tray with steel wool.

'Yeah, after being in the studio all day... the fresh air... ah, the fresh air.' Ger comes up behind me, slipping his arm around my waist. He's wearing the wax jacket he takes with him on the boat. I can smell the impregnated wax.

'You were out a good while.' My body remains rigid.

'I love it out there, with the sea, my muse...'

'Did you have a drink?'

'Just a glass of wine on the way home. I might run a bath. Do you mind sorting those out?'

'That's grand.'

'You're the best.' He kisses me hard on the neck.

I heard the bath water drain down the pipes twenty minutes ago. On the worktop are the six mackerel that I presume are shop bought. I turn one over, looking at its eyes, its rainbow skin. I glance at the paintings above the bins; the cloudy eyed fish, like us all, just guts inside. I lift the bowl out of the sink and turn on the cold tap.

I slice through the first fish's neck and I realise that the fish were purchased at nine in the morning when the boats came in. Ger would've told the fishmonger not to fillet them, storing them in the gallery fridge. I find myself hacking at the fish's heads as the idea of him buying the fish in the morning sinks in.

The six fish lie on the chopping board; I toss their heads into the bin. My hands are coated in oils that no amount of scrubbing can get clean. One by one, I slice the mackerel open and drag their spines out. I lay the knife down.

I pause but then I pick it up again. I hold the knife down by my side, safety first, like I taught Lorcan. I walk towards the stairs. I take each step quietly, passing by Ger's large seascapes, ignoring the froth of their waves. Upstairs, the bathroom light has been left on, the door open.

Our bedroom door is ajar; I can hear the faint sound of his snore. I walk in, lightly pushing back the door. Ger doesn't move, his left hand lounged across my side of the bed. I stand over him, the knife hovering an inch from his throat. My hand is steady. I pause, wondering can I make the slice, knowing my son is only two doors away. Yet even with the thought of Lorcan, I cannot draw my hand away, caught between action and retreat.

I notice the reflection of his throat on the stainless steel – the beginnings of a rash caused by his bath time shave. The skin is red and blotchy, exposing the raw flesh underneath. My knife pulls away. Tonight I won't kill my husband. I realise that for sixteen hours a day he may be an artist living beyond the rules, who can sail across the ocean to find a muse or fuck some bitch, but for eight hours a night, I know he sleeps like the rest of us, a snoring bag of meat. And if I wanted I could slit his throat and gut him like a fish.

THE BELIEVER

'...to prove our almost-instinct almost true:
What will survive of us is love.'

Philip Larkin, 'An Arundel Tomb'

I crawl up the icy tiles, my damp socks slipping on the glassy surface. It is eight a.m. on the seventh of March, a Saturday, and the pale dawn has already begun. Though my haze is drug induced, I sense the danger of my predicament. I stuff my unopened beer in my back pocket and lean into the ridges, my numb fingers clinging to the lead and concrete. I hope I won't break a tile. I pray I won't slip downwards off the three storeys to my death.

Below, Wayne stands on a barstool on the balcony, gazing up at the rooftop. He waits for me to clamber onto the peak and sit down on the triangular point. I click open my beer can. He lifts his body onto the tiles, his torso scraping off the white gutter; ice and cobwebs streak up his T-shirt. I watch as he positions his bottle of Carlsberg between his teeth, freeing his right hand. He shakes his head so that the rosary beads, presumably bought in River Island, unhook themselves from his chin. I fear that he might fall. But he looks at me and grins. Perhaps he has made this journey before.

He is blond, late-twenties and good looking, though his looks are boyish, tied into his youth. I don't know him well; he is a figure who has flickered in and out of my life, appearing at moments when I'm trying to escape reality. He tries to stand as he climbs, making his predicament more precarious. I urge him not to risk it. His striped purple socks fail to grip the tiles, forcing him onto his knees. It is only as he sits beside me that I notice his lower arm is cut; a large black-green smudge frames a line of glistening crimson blood.

He ignores it and takes a swig from the bottle, stretching his legs along the rooftop. I gaze down the slope toward Sunday's Well; beyond a group of houses is an ancient limestone church. I can see its front courtyard, spying the grey shadows where the white ice covers the ground thickly. There is a sign on the lawn; I can't read it but I imagine it asks visitors not to stand on the grass. The sun is yet to pass over the horizon but the navy sky has given way to turquoise, soft pinks and lemons. I know that it will be a beautiful day in Cork but for now it is cold and already my feet are growing numb. The city in the valley below is silent. So silent, in fact, I wonder does the coldness itself have a discernible white noise. Or maybe it is an echo from clubbing the night before.

I see Wayne's breath fog as he blows it out, like smoke. He places the bottle between his thighs and folds his arms together. My feet and fingers ache, but I enjoy the clarity the frost gives my mind. My fatigue vanishes.

Wayne gets out his cameraphone and takes a number of shots. They are grainy; the light is not bright enough. Dark shadows filter out from the corners of my eyes. We are ghosts almost, shadows and indistinct form. I delete the worst of the pictures, saving a shot of our faces surrounded by blue-grey sky and another of our legs stretching over the glistening tiles towards the gutter. Our feet look small compared to the sky, the horizon, even the rooftop. I remember a song by Goldfrapp, though I don't mention it; it sounds almost too contrived to say the lyrics. Instead I say,

'You know, when they looked in my granddad's pockets, they found my Australian number and his dog's licence.'

Wayne squeezes my shoulder and we talk for a while longer. I am rambling. Wayne probably won't recall it. He'll just remember the roof, the photograph, the numbness creeping into his toes till he can feel each individual bone as it moves, and it becomes inevitable that we must go inside the house.

I am back from Sydney less than a month. I had not planned to be home.

In the front garden of Ashgrove Cottage there are a number of plastic birds sprouting up out of the ground; some are sky-blue, some are yellow, others plain white. They hover above the primroses and snowdrops, their wings spinning like propellers whenever a gust of wind blows over the laurel hedges. I am not sure if they are ugly or beautiful.

Though the main road by the cottage has got progressively busier, a low grey pebbledash wall has been wired to hold roses and honeysuckle, guarding the house from the worst of the dust. The gate is closed as Granddad owns dogs that seem to have a thirst for danger and fast cars. I pick at the wire mesh between the metal bars, which has been pinned on to keep the dogs inside and allow only their barks to escape the garden's confines. My father warns me to watch my fingers.

The two Jack Russells, Miley and Tiny, poke their noses through the mesh. I don't like Miley, who is pale brown, watery-eyed and snappy. Tiny, on the other hand, is smart, a typical Jack Russell with brown and black spots, intelligent eyes and an ability to go from zero to sixty in an instant. His only flaw is his incessant barking, which causes Granddad occasionally to lift his cap and slap the dog on the backside with it.

The cottage itself is small, painted off-white with a slate roof and small wooden-framed windows. Either side of a central pathway are raised flowerbeds with old-fashioned roses and among them sit home-made jam-jar traps to catch the wasps. In one of the flower beds is a birdbath; Granddad has a great fear of petty thievery so it has a large rock on top of it.

Granddad walks up the path and opens the gate.

'Will you give your aul Granddad a birdie?' he asks Aoife and me. I refuse to give him a kiss on the cheek. Shortly after my parents leave, Granddad makes us lunch; through the open front door I can hear the radio. Aoife kicks the silver tray at the bottom of the gutter with her jelly sandals, watching the dirt rise, clouding the water. I pick up a stick, lift out pieces of moss and rotting leaves, and flick them at her. I dare her to stick her foot into the water. She is hesitant but after my teasing she lifts up her sandal and splashes it in the tray.

'Aoife! You dirty thing.' Nana is standing in the porch doorway. 'And put down that stick before you hurt yourself.'

Aoife raises the stick high, waving it. Nana pushes out her bottom lip and pretends to cry.

'You wouldn't hit your poor old Nan.'

'I would, Nana – I would,' my sister replies, her face earnest.

'You'd hit poor Nana?'

'I would, I'd belt you with it.'

The stand-off continues until Granddad appears.

'Stop that blaggarding now,' he says to Aoife. 'Your poor Nan.'

Aoife turns red.

'We won't have any tears now,' he says. 'Come in here.' We go inside. Granddad gives us Silvermints, and puts Aoife's wet sandal in front of the fire. Nana goes back to bed to rest and he brings her in a cup of tea along with her tablets.

We sit on the settee, moving the yellowing *Avondhu* newspapers and tea towels. Aoife strokes Tiny while I look around. The walls are covered with faded photographs and hooks full of rusty keys, all coated in opaque cobwebs. I ask Granddad why he doesn't clean them off.

'They kill the flies,' he replies. He's making us 'pandy' – buttery potato mash – on a hotplate.

'What about the germs?' Aoife asks.

'Isn't there enough of us about? A few germs never harmed anyone.'

'Who are they Granddad?' she then asks. I know she is aware of the answer. Above the cluttered mantelpiece there are two circular pictures in gold frames, one of a blonde girl, the other of a brown-haired boy.

'Sure, that's you and Conor,' he replies. Aoife smiles.

I watch as Granddad takes down a tin of tea and scoops a number of spoons into the pot. His hands shake a little. He butters some bread, placing the slices directly on the counter, and licks the knife. I find this strange; my mother would slap my knife away if I attempted it.

'Who's that?' I ask. There is a large picture on the wall, above photographs of my father's first wedding, and those of my two aunts, Bridget and Kate. The print is a portrait of a couple I don't recognise that has faded with daylight.

'That's the Kennedys. By God, all your questions! Sure, the Guards wouldn't ask me that.' He smiles at us. His face is heavily worn from thirty years in the Forestry.

We devour the sausages and pandy. Granddad opens the Mikado biscuits. I take one and drag my finger along its centre, scooping out the pink jam, pulling off the marshmallow. Granddad lets us finish the packet.

I watch as he rinses the cutlery in the sink, the hot water coming from a white heater that's fixed to the wall. Using a cupped right hand, in a move I've seen him repeat often, he brushes the crumbs on the table together and off the side into his left palm, before tossing them into the sink where they wash away.

Later, we stand by the car and Granddad places silver coins in our hands. 'Put that in your pocket,' he says and we thank him. I turn the coins, my fingers scratching the rough edges, contemplating what sweets I might buy though I'm still full from lunch.

He has just paid us for berries that he does not want, which we picked from his own garden. Though there are some blackcurrants in the old ice-cream tub, most of its contents are gooseberries. They are larger and easier to pick, but diseased, laced with a brown-grey fungus. I think about Stinger and Refresher bars.

Nana walks to the car, her movements slow. She is dressed in a smart tweed jacket with a Celtic broach on the lapel. Her thick hair is pinned across her forehead, crimped to one side. Though in her sixties, much of her hair is still raven. Granddad opens the door of the red Morris Minor as her hands are stiff, cupped inwards with arthritis.

He lifts his seat up so that we can jump in the back. The car smells of dust and newspaper ink. Granddad insists we fasten our belts. He slowly nudges out onto the road, asking can we see any traffic. I look at the swinging bronze fish that hangs from the mirror and the cross on the dashboard stuck down with Bluetac. Once outside, Granddad tucks the car into the pavement, hops out and closes the gate. He checks the front door a second time.

I pick a pamphlet off the back seat. On the reverse I see the proposed routes for the new Castlemoy bypass. I say that it'd be great to get a bypass in the town with all the traffic passing through it. I have heard grown-ups talk like this – polite conversations about roads and weather. Nana humours me.

Nana waits in the car while Granddad takes us into Hickey's. Behind the counter are rows of five- and ten-pence bars. I've no intention of buying just one bar of Cadbury's chocolate and a packet of Taytos. Instead my thoughts are on how I might buy as many sweets as possible. My mouth waters at the sight of Desperate Dans, chewy orange gum laced with black sherbet. There are ten-pence corn crisps, the kind that get stuck in my teeth, sherbet dips in the shape of pencils, cola bottles and flying saucers. In the end, I buy three Refreshers, two Desperate Dans, twenty penny sweets, Meanies and a Sherbet Dip. I watch carefully what Aoife buys, not wanting her to make better choices. I hope she won't see a sweet that I've missed; jealousy might ruin what I already have.

I cling onto the small plastic bag that holds my sweets. Now that I am satisfied, I find Granddad at the rear of the shop. He has a basket with an uncut loaf of white bread in it. He picks five packets of pink wafers off the biscuit stand, along with a packet of Mikado. I watch as he lifts up a pound of Dairygold. 'Mam buys Flora; it's healthier,' I tell him as I dip the liquorice into the sherbet. He says nothing, just listens to my chatter. My fingers are stained purple-black from the berry picking. Aoife joins us with her bag of sweets.

Finally, Granddad places two chocolate éclairs on top of the basket. We pass by the freezer. He says we can pick out an ice cream. Aoife picks out a Triple Chocolate Magnum which is over two pounds. He laughs.

We pass the fruit and vegetable stand. Granddad doesn't stop.

'Don't you want some fruit, Granddad?' I ask.

Granddad gives the bananas a withering stare.

'They'd cut the stomach off ya.'

At the counter he buys a packet of Silk Cut Purple for Nana. I'd like to smoke, having pretended at school. I quite like the smell of it, the same way petrol smells very good at the garage, before it causes a headache. I ask Granddad if he smokes. He had a pipe, he says, but he gave it up. He doesn't say why. Though young, I realise not to ask more questions. Granddad tells what he wants to tell; the rest he brushes off with a joke. He gives a twenty pound note to the lady; again I notice his hand has a tremor but it doesn't seem to bother him.

In the car, Nana asks if we like our sweets. We say yes and thank her; there's silence as Granddad drives to the top of the village and turns around. We pass Grindell's Pub on the way out of the village; it has a famous traditional front used on placemats and calendars. I ask Granddad if he drinks there, knowing his answer. He tells us that he drank fifteen pints of Guinness the night before and picked a fight with a tinker. We laugh. Granddad has been a pioneer his whole life.

To the west of Ashgrove Cottage the sun dips behind the line of conifers. I finish my last Desperate Dan. I am soaked up to my knees, wading through the dewy grass at the back of the cottage. Across the garden, the grass is littered with old pieces of galvanise and nettles. I see a rope swinging from side to side under the conifers, though Aoife is hidden as the line of ancient gooseberry bushes blocks my view.

I glance upwards and see Nana's bedroom window. The house is higher at the back, as the land drops away here. She never looks out. All I can see is the faint gold fringe of a lampshade; above it is a yellowing blind and a piece of cord hanging down from the centre. The pebble-dash is a soft grey, though as it nears ground it turns to shades of green. A rusting white cooker lies abandoned in the long grass.

Granddad rarely comes around the back of the cottage; unlike the front, where the hedges are trimmed into clean lines, here the laurel splays out in unruly fronds. I play by the apple tree, its low thick branches twisted and covered in knots. It's laden with cooking apples that are no longer picked; the bulbous thick-skinned fruit lies scattered in the tufts of grass, riddled with holes from flies and worms.

I sit on the damp stick, the rope rising from between my legs, and I push off. The branch dips with my weight. Above, I can see where the rope has torn the bark from the branch. As I swing out further, I reach beyond the flattened grass under the swing, kicking the heads off nettles, confident in my thick jeans.

In the field, Tiny picks individual blades of grass and chews them methodically, an occasional splutter coming from his throat. His face is one of great concentration, his body perfectly still as, stem by stem, he makes himself vomit. I feel sick after my sweets, though I would still eat more. I know Aoife still has a packet of Wine Gums that she will tease me with, eating them one by one in front of me.

The evening is setting in. I know it won't be long before our parents arrive. Aoife appears from the far side of the field. She has a plan to make an apple pie. We ignore the rotten apples on the ground, reaching for the largest fruit that weigh down the branches. Some of the skins break away from the fruit as we yank them off. I chase Aoife with the rotten juice covering my fingertips, threatening to touch her hair.

She dares me to bite into an apple. I glance at the high window of Nana's bedroom. Granddad has already warned us the apples would make us sick. But not to be considered a chicken (Aoife having already stuck her sandal in the silver tub), I take a bite of the fruit. It is dry and horribly sour like the gooseberries so I spit it out.

Having witnessed my mother baking apple pie, we know the apples have to be cored. I remember the abandoned Morris Minor in the furthest part of the garden. It is tangled with briars and weeds. I flick up the metal window wiper and push the apple down onto its point and twist. White and brown flesh trickle out from the apple's centre onto the bonnet.

I grow confident with each apple I core. I forget that the apples are for a cake, enjoying instead the destruction of the overripe fruit against the sharp metal. My hands grow sticky with clear juice as pips and seeds glide down the wiper into the grill. I sit higher up on the rusting bonnet and it dips under my weight. Aoife brings me more apples riddled with holes and smudged with dirt.

I hammer the next apple down on the rusty point but the rotten core slides too easily and the sharp point pierces the centre of my palm. I pull away with a shout of pain, blood pouring out of the wound, dripping onto the bonnet. Aoife screams, shouting for Granddad. I place my hand onto my mouth and the taste of metal hits my tongue.

We run up the garden, dragging our feet over the long

grass. Aoife is two steps in front, calling for help. I feel dizzy as I lurch through the side gate, past the Victorian roses and trimmed laurel, to the cottage entrance.

Granddad is at the door; he lifts me onto a chair so I can reach over the sink and cold water can flow over the wound. As the blood drains away, I can see it is not as deep as I imagined; the wiper has not pierced right through my hand. Granddad opens a cabinet and lifts out a small purple tincture bottle. I frown; it is neither Savlon nor a Band-Aid. He drips it onto a piece of torn cloth and cleans the wound. It stings. Later, I discover that he has used iodine.

My wound is bandaged; I sit by Nana's bed and she feeds me Silvermints from the three half-open packets that she has on the bedside locker, beside some rosary beads, purple Silk Cut and her pink-framed glasses. Above the bed is a long wall heater, the tangerine bar radiating heat onto the right side of my face. I gaze at the high wooden ceiling and mention the dust that must come through the cracks, a comment I have heard my mother make. Nana doesn't answer, but offers me another mint.

Once the tears have subsided, and the pain in my hand has calmed down to a warn throb, I ask Nana about the scar on her forehead, just about her left eyebrow. It is a roundish mark, rather like a burn. She says she got it from a thorn on a rosebush, touching the mark gently, before rousing herself and changing the subject.

We stop at a garage and pick up Silvermints and pink wafers. Mallow hospital is the next turn on the left. I drive slowly, the black conifers on each side slipping by, leaving the road in shade. It is easy to miss the narrow turn-off, which leads up the hill between the trees.

The hospital is imposing, sitting high up on a slope, a relic from the age of monasteries and convents. The car must go under an old limestone arch, over which the Cork-Dublin train travels once an hour. As we pass through it, I realise the arch is a doorway of sorts, beyond which one encounters the fundamentals of life – birth, death, health and sickness.

Granddad has been in hospital for three days. I have not been able to visit him till now. Each day we are told he will go home the following morning. But on the third day I feel anxious. My instinct tells me that for some old people a hospital visit is routine, but for a man who has not been admitted to hospital in over sixty years, a visit is a dangerous thing.

He could easily live to one hundred, despite the fact that he has prophesied his death annually for twenty years, assuring us he will not survive another winter. Yet he has remained unchanged through those two decades. It seems he became an old man at a young age, before pausing time so that everyone else caught up with him and then passed him out.

But his eldest daughter, my aunt Kate, is dying of cancer. She will die, as sure as Nana died of cancer. From the moment I heard Kate was ill, I have sensed that Granddad will not outlive her. I cannot envisage him at her funeral. Yet this is not for any definite reason; we are told he is simply dehydrated.

The only space is in the lowest car park. Stepping out of the car, I wrap my coat up tightly. We climb the steps to the hospital. My feet are numb, my Converse doing little to keep them warm.

'He was brighter last night,' Aoife says.

'Hopefully, he still is' I reply, slightly breathless.

It is bright in the clearing by the hospital, though there's a wind gusting. By the time we reach the entrance, I can see my sister's cheeks are flushed. I have not been to this hospital in over a decade, since Nana was sick. It is unchanged from the outside at least. The thick walls have a smooth quality that makes me think there are numerous layers of paint underneath, which would read like the rings of a tree.

We step inside the reception and the air changes; warm but stale, as if I'm not the first to breathe it. There's a faint smell from an unseen hospital canteen. I ask for Granddad and we go to St Mary's ward. We clean our hands on the alcohol dispensers; the winter vomiting bug is taking its toll. Bridget, my other aunt, is in the corridor.

'The doctor is in to see him,' she says. 'He isn't so good today.'

I hug her, though it is awkward. I am not the hugging sort, nor is she. We talk about him while nurses move around us.

'I don't understand it,' Bridget says. 'He was much brighter yesterday, blaggarding away, as you know.'

I smile at her choice of words.

'Is he on medication?' Aoife asks.

'They have him on antibiotics. Yesterday they thought it might be pneumonia.'

Bridget asks about her sister. Kate is home from the hospital. There is nothing else they can do. She is too weak for chemotherapy, but they hope she might regain enough strength to fight a little longer. We shake our heads and feel helpless. There are few words available that can offer comfort. I know Bridget has her faith, her rosary and her church. I have my faith also, though in what exactly I am unsure.

The doctor appears, a textbook doctor, middle-aged and healthy, with a thick head of pepper-and-salt hair. He looks grave and asks to speak to my aunt alone. Even though I will not be in the room to hear the words, I know what will be said.

My aunt is crying when she comes out. I have never seen her cry; like Granddad, she is the practical 'just get on with it' sort. She shakes her head at me and I hug her for almost a full minute. She pulls away and says,

'He's not responding to the antibiotics.' She dabs her red eyes with a tissue, her smooth cheeks flushed. She has my Nana's skin, unlined even in her forties. 'The doctor said to prepare ourselves. His heart is weak. He probably won't survive the night.'

The words make me feel dizzy. I don't know what to say.

'Can we go into him?' Aoife asks; her eyes are glassy.

'Yes, but just prepare yourselves. He's not what he was.'

We walk into the ward which is full of old men, mouths open as they struggle to breathe. Granddad's bed is blocked by a curtain; I fear what I'll see.

As I look around the curtain I realise that my aunt is right; he's not what he was. For the first time in a quarter of a century, he seems truly different. An oxygen mask covers part of his gaunt face, his false teeth are removed and his eyes are glassy. Yet he knows who we are and I'm grateful for that.

We talk for a while. He's breathless but attempts to sit up and we help him into position. His eyes focus better; it seems he'll be himself for a little while.

'Will you give your old granddad a birdie?' he asks Aoife. She kisses his cheek.

'I enjoyed our lunch the other week,' I say to him. 'That dinner was well worth coming back from Australia for, despite the queer company.'

103

'I was delighted to see you,' he says, looking directly into my eyes. The effort exhausts him. I take a deep breath and touch his hand, wanting him to know I love him but fearing the words would sound ridiculous. On his arm there is my Nana's watch, gold with a patent black leather strap. Her thin wedding band fits on his baby finger.

'You'll have to get better now,' Bridget says. 'The dog's missing you.'

Granddad smiles at the mention of the new puppy. He scratches his chest, the sticky pads irritating his skin. I notice he has hair on his chest; I realise for the first time he is a man. He has an identity other than 'Granddad'.

'Did you have any lunch?' my aunt then asks. I see a look in Granddad's eye.

'Sure the Pope wouldn't ask me that,' he smiles. He continues pulling at the white circles on his chest, peeling one off and rolling it in his fingers. I glance at Aoife but I say nothing. Instead I speak of our previous lunch. He'd commented on my shoes. 'They're a grand pair, Conor. Do they match? Are they the same shoe at all?' he'd said. I could see that familiar mischievous look in his eyes.

'No, they're different, Granddad,' I'd replied. 'One's a left and one's a right.'

Our hospital visit lasts till the nurse says we have to leave. It's dinner time. I know the rest of the family will come in the evening. I want to stay, knowing this will be the last time I see him as himself. Just as we are leaving a blonde nurse brings him food. He says to her,

'Did you meet my grandson?'

I smile, embarrassed. The nurse has brought him a banana smoothie to eat. My aunt feeds him two mouthfuls. His face turns. I ask if he would rather have some tea and toast instead.

'Don't bring me nothing,' he says, getting annoyed. The nurse looks flustered. Then he winks at me.

We stay at the hospital for the night, waiting for notice that Granddad's condition had changed, so we can join our aunt and be with him as he breathes his last. Aoife and I are in a visitors' room, away from the drunks in Accident and Emergency. The room is comfortable, very warm, with a television that has only three channels. The seats are large; big, flowery cushions on wicker bases, like furniture from someone's conservatory.

I've slept for five hours. My neck is stiff from sleeping upright. I am thirsty from the hot room, the coffee and the packaged sandwiches. The battery in my phone is dead. I sit still, not wanting to wake my sister, experiencing the contradictory feelings of fatigue and alertness. It is growing light outside. I tease open the curtain an inch and see that the sky is clear. The stars are fading, the navy slipping into hues of orange and light blue.

I close my eyes, willing more sleep, but after ten minutes of arranging my coat as a pillow, it is clear that I will not drift off. Five hours will be my lot. I lift out my iPod. My usual music annoys me; in fact, all singing is too much. I wish I had downloaded something classical.

I scroll down the touch screen looking for something that is bearable. I have a meditation track, which I try to listen to but the man narrating the visualisation has an irritating accent. I find it impossible to connect to the image of an abandoned beach.

My eyes stop on Goldfrapp. When their latest album had been initially released it'd been too quiet for me. However, in Australia I'd grown to enjoy it, walking through Sydney's Hyde Park on the way to work, listening to *Seventh Tree* as the sun rose. I decide to play it, enjoying the understated folk-inspired tunes, enjoying Alison Goldfrapp's breathy vocals. I flick to the songs I like – 'A&E' and 'Happiness' – before listening to the remainder of the album.

The sky outside is growing brighter. I lift the curtain again, this time a little wider. Though the sun has yet to pass over the roof of the hospital wing opposite, the navy sky has gone. It is now all turquoise, soft pinks and lemons. It has been a good spring; this type of dawn has been repeated often and, I imagine, will occur again. The tiles on the buildings are white with ice. I imagine my breath turning to fog if I were to step outside.

Aoife wakes up. We talk a little, though the bustle earlier in the night has given way to a tired silence. I drink some of her bottled water and ask if she has a mint. At that moment, a nurse comes into the room, looking awkward,

'I'm sorry but your grandfather has died,' she says. 'Your aunt is down in the hallway.'

I glance at Aoife. I can see her eyes turn glassy. There can be no turning back. I hug her, then pick up my coat from the seat and slip it on, even though I'm already too warm. We go down to the main corridor; Bridget is there. She cries when she sees us. She says he went quietly and he was in no pain. I'm upset that the nurse waited until he died before telling us. I would've liked to hold his hand at the end.

We are directed to the canteen. It's closed but the nurse allows us inside. I silently make tea and pick a fruit scone from the stainless steel stand. We say little, just a comment or two about our lack of knowledge about organising funerals.

The large windows allow a view of the rising sun. I can see the ice on the cars and grass outside. The sun's pale rays hit the roofs. Beyond the canteen, dim noises from Accident and

Emergency echo through. Each of us glances at the others. I don't know whether I should mention heaven and say 'he's gone to a better place'. Truth is, I'm not sure of it.

The nurse returns after twenty minutes and tells us we can go and see Granddad. Rousing myself, I place my cup onto the small white plate, along with the knife and teaspoon. My aunt takes them. Yet as she pulls away, I notice crumbs on the table and ask her to wait, instinctively cupping my hands, brushing the crumbs together and off the side of the table into my left palm. I pause, aware of my movements. For a brief moment I am comforted.

We enter the hospital ward and I can see the drawn curtains around Granddad's bed. The nurse lets us slip in behind them. I have never believed in a soul, but if I did perhaps this would be the strongest proof. I look at a body, small, mouth still open, but it isn't him. Everything that I recognise about him is gone. His face isn't rosy, rather waxed. His eyes, perhaps his most defining feature, are closed and calm. My aunt kisses his forehead. I am scared to touch him as I am fearful he will be cold – another proof that he is gone.

On the bedside sits a bottle of holy water and a rosary. My aunt tells me he received his last rites. Though I have always considered it superstition, I am comforted by the ritual; not because I feel Granddad needs forgiveness from God, but because this is what he wanted.

We stand in silence, looking at him. The nurses have put in his false teeth. The duvet has been pulled up around his neck. We are tired so it is hard to process emotions. They come out as quiet tears and disbelief. I think of how much I want him to be alive. I want the walls of family pictures in Ashgrove Cottage to hold my next photograph, whatever it is, to have it hang next to my graduation pictures. Yet it is too much to ask someone to live for me alone.

I know there was nothing that could've been done. When I consider that his will to live was so strong that Time itself had conceded, allowing him total independence (he lived alone, still driving in his mid-eighties and without any real sickness), it became impossible to imagine how anyone could influence him once his will to live had become a choice to die. My aunt is thinking similarly. She says,

'Two weeks ago he asked me to get his best suit dry-cleaned. He said "you never know when I might be needing it".'

'Bridget put his cap and a photograph of the Jack Russells in his coffin,' I say, gazing at my feet, unable to look at Wayne directly. I squeeze my toes; the joints ache with cold.

I feel embarrassed that I've cried and been so open with Wayne about Granddad's death and my childhood, which would never have appeared so perfect if it were not for the love he showed me and Aoife. I know that my rambling might never have happened without the drugs and alcohol. But maybe this was the way it was meant to be, that I would sit on a rooftop and talk about Granddad's kindness, this being the only sort of life after death I could be sure of.

I breathe in deeply, looking out at the dawn. The warm pastel shades are still there but growing fainter as the sky becomes a proper blue. I glance eastward, waiting for the moment the sun might appear above the line of trees.

'How's your aunt Kate doing?' Wayne asks.

'She died a couple of days after Granddad,' I say. My throat feels tight. I blink a few times to stop the tears forming. After a few moments I rouse myself. 'How's your arm anyhow?'

'A bit sore but I don't think it'll scar,' Wayne says, trying to scrape off the powdery green moss with his fingernail. 'It hasn't bled too much.'

I glance down at the palm of my right hand; the scar that was once there is gone, lost in the maze of lines that possibly predict the course of my own life. Do I believe in that? I don't know. Maybe I do almost-believe in something more, or at least want to.

'Christ, it's cold,' Wayne says finally. 'You want to get down and have another line?'

I resist saying yes. It feels unlikely that I will take more coke, for now anyway. I begin to sense that this particular moment, this intermittent friendship which has led me to climb a roof with Wayne will return to the near non-existence that it was before. I'll most likely go home and behave sensibly and he'll forget most of what I've said, while the bit he does remember he'll pass off and forgive. We might meet again at some point. Then again, we might not.

'Yeah, maybe we should head in,' I say, knowing I can make my excuses once we're inside. I tuck the empty bottle into my trouser pocket and begin to descend the tiles, feeling steadier than before, slipping down from the roof onto the chair on the balcony. I watch as he inches down, half-sliding in his purple socks.

But as he reaches for the gutter, the swinging rosary beads get caught on his thumb. The cheap plastic snaps and the beads scatter down the tiles, rattling like marbles. I try to catch them but they fall everywhere, into the drains and plant pots, and around the legs of the wooden table and chairs. A few others escape, slipping through the gaps in the balcony railings, dropping like crumbs, lost forever in the ice that lies below.

THAT AMPLE PAST

'It's gorgeous.' Mer walks around the study.

'It needs loads of work.' I glance at the stacks of books that require shelving. But there are years ahead to be thinking about shelves.

'I love the high ceiling,' Ruth says. She peers out the blinds. 'It's west-facing?'

'Yes; it gets the sun in the evening.' I try to ignore the crack in the wall by the window. I know neither of them will mention it but I'm certain Ruth will see it. Once an interior designer, it would be as natural for her to see a crack on a wall as it would be for me to find a misplaced comma on a page.

'So this is where the magic will happen,' Mer touches the reclaimed oak desk, 'where manuscripts will be stacked and sorted?'

'Something like that.'

'You never know – you might go back to it yourself.'

I smile. Now thirty, my writing no longer feels necessary. It was a therapy that helped me through the tricky age of young adulthood. Granted, a couple of my stories were published; one was even shortlisted at the Listowel Festival. But then I found a job that I quite liked, friends I enjoyed spending weekends with, and I felt reconciled with my past. 'I've been weeded out,' I say, quoting a professor who'd given an introductory speech on my first day in University College Dublin:

'Some of you are writers. Most of you are book-lovers – readers in fact. Because the difference between a writer and a reader is a writer actually writes.'

It seemed like an obvious statement at the time but over the following years his words were proved right – though twelve of us completed the Master's in Creative Writing, only three became writers. We all loved books and no doubt read extensively, working in the arts as journalists, editors, administrators and teachers. But Time had weeded out the readers from the writers.

'I thought you hated ornaments.' Mer picks up a carving of a monk that sits on the desk, a prize from a flash-fiction competition.

'They seem to find me,' I reply, picking a circular gold frame out of a box; it contains a picture of a small boy. Truth is, I don't think of these objects as ornaments as they are not simply decorative. They're artefacts from my past. Each contains a memory that transforms them into a type of talisman. I know that when I die my nieces and nephews will clear out this house that I've just bought, glance at the assortment of objects that I see as priceless, see nothing of value and fling most of it into a skip. Their hidden energies will die with me, as I'm the only person who knows about them. Of course, my relatives will keep a few things aside, artefacts for their own accumulating archaeology, charged with a whole new type of energy. And that would be enough.

'Who's this from?' Ruth lifts up a framed musical score, reading the dedication. She wipes away the fine layer of dust on the glass, and tucks her smooth black hair behind her ear.

'It was a gift from a composer I once knew. I've had it years.' By saying that I've had it a long time, I'm attempting to deflect the true story. This is not because I believe Ruth or Mer will judge; it's an instinctive response arising from the fact that Ruth has children who are nearly my age. Truth be told, the score is from the summer of my twenty-fifth birthday when I spent idle afternoons fucking a nineteen-year-old music student. I wasn't working – the recession had seen to that. Yet it wasn't just fucking; we had a semi-relationship. I'd stay after we'd both cum, sitting naked on his small bed while he played the piano.

'Have you composed anything?' I asked him once.

'Just messing around. I've nothing on paper.' And as he played, I noticed the acne on his shoulders, a proof of his youth, vital and unapologetic.

'But what if you died tomorrow?' I said, sitting forward, flicking a condom wrapper onto the floor. 'You must write things down – inspiration goes if you don't look after it.'

'I will,' he replied but there was uncertainty in his voice.

'If you don't have something written by next time, we're not fucking.'

He smiled, too young to have something clever to say in reply. I kissed him. Perhaps that was what the muses of old had to do – barter sex so that the reluctant and lazy geniuses would work.

At the end of the summer, he asked if we could be together.

'You're nineteen,' I replied. 'Forget about me, focus on your music and fuck around for at least a decade – then you'll be a composer.'

'So who was he, this composer?' Mer asks.

I open the fridge door, lifting out chicken breasts and curry paste.

'An ingénu,' I reply. 'It's a gorgeous song, kind of like the music from Amélie. Did you get a glass of wine? What about the champagne – d'you think it's chilled?'

'Can I help with anything?' Ruth asks. Scattered across the worktop are bags and tins of ingredients. I know I'm being ambitious making a three-course dinner but I want it to be impressive.

'Not at all. Sit down there now and don't be stressing. I've everything under control. Excuse the crap everywhere.'

If I'm honest, I'm apologising but not actually embarrassed. I'm proud of my new home; I know that one day the laminate floor in the kitchen will be granite tiles and the white electric oven will be chrome. The pea-green bathroom suite will be removed and replaced by an antique bath with four legs and matching fixtures.

'When does David get in?' Ruth asks.

'He'll be here any minute; his last supervision is at four. You'll have to excuse me; cooking is the one thing I can't do and talk at the same time. I could polish the house, hoover… anything. Just not cooking.'

I cut the mangetout, thinking about David. I'm reminded of Michael Cunningham's *The Hours* and wonder have I transformed from Richard into Clarissa; there were times in my life when I might've chosen to live in a more dazzling but dangerous way, but now it seems likely that I'll fuck the same man for the foreseeable future and live sensibly, safe and unnoticed by brilliance or disaster.

I'm happy to be unnoticed and I've never felt like this before. Though I loved the process of writing – typing on my laptop for hours was the only way to be sure a day wasn't wasted – the ego was never entirely separate from this desire. I'd wanted success and acclaim; there were critics from my past who needed silencing. Maybe that was all the impulse to write ever was, a wish to prove myself; and now that I was content, the drive was gone.

I wonder if I should ask David to move in with me; we've only been together nine months but he is dependable. In fact, I suspect the biggest danger to our relationship is me, that I might revert to a former incarnation. But this seems less and less likely.

I glance over my shoulder, watching as Mer teases the cork out of the champagne bottle.

'Christ, you're an expert at that. Your Nana taught you well,' I laugh. Mer and I have often spoken of our grandparents; her grandmother spent her final years wearing pearls and well-cut suits, and drinking champagne. Mer hands me a wine glass. 'I'll have proper glasses next time.'

'Would you look at her,' Ruth says, lifting up a copy of the *Irish Independent Weekend* magazine, showing a picture of a former Irish model who's written a book.

'That… at the National Book Awards!' Mer exclaims. 'What was she thinking?'

'It's probably stuffed full of coke,' I say, glancing at the pink wig. 'Honest to God, I should've just married a rugby player. I'd be on my sixth book by now.' I take a large mouthful of champagne. I make a point of never criticising people who have finished a novel because it is an achievement in itself to have the discipline to get one hundred thousand words on paper. Yet there are moments – books that are littered with adverbs, authors who achieve book deals as a result of sleeping with an athlete, so-called writers with slashes in their career profile (model/presenter/reality TV star/ children's writer) – which leaves me sorely tempted to break this resolution.

My phone beeps; it's David, asking if I need him to pick up anything. As I text back, asking for an extra carton of custard and a box of After Eights, I wonder how he sees me and, in a wider sense, how the friends of my latter youth perceive me. Would David or the others have recognised me a decade ago? I've never told them about the time I auditioned, underage, on a TV music show and was told that, though I looked good on camera, I couldn't hold a note if I tried. Nor have I told them about the awkwardness I experienced after I fooled around with one of my straight mates when we were both high on coke. Granted, these were old stories from my late teens and early twenties, memories I'd rather forget; but would my more recent friends think so well of me if they knew these things had happened?

My cheeks flush and I throw the onion and chicken into the pan. I hear Mer talking to Ruth about a new poetry anthology that she's reviewed for *The Irish Times*.

'It was good, just too long,' she says. 'He should've cut it down a bit. Nobody needs one hundred and thirty pages of poetry. But there was one beautiful line…'

I turn the chicken and onions; the cloudy pink flesh turns solid white in patches. It seems incredible that I have such friends, one who writes reviews for *The Irish Times*, the other a winner of the Orange Prize. Would they think less of me if I wasn't such an edited version of my original foolish self?

The chicken is cooked; I add the mangetout and peas, and open the cans of coconut milk. I decide I'll continue with my deception; after all, the more I live the lie, the more likely it will become permanent truth.

The starter is tasty but unimpressive; a selection of spring rolls, wontons and satay chicken skewers from Marks & Spencer, cooked from frozen, giving me time to leave the green curry to simmer and stir in the lemongrass, soy and coriander. I wish I could serve the curry in nicer bowls, possibly square-shaped, rather than the round breakfast ones.

'I wouldn't have a clue how to make it this well,' Mer says about the curry. 'A jar is about the best I can manage.'

I lift the homemade apple crumble from the oven and heat the custard. I hear Owen and Mark, Ruth and Mer's respective partners, talking loudly about the trial of a former Minister's lover. There are two empty bottles of wine sitting beside the recycling bin.

'She shouldn't have taken the money,' Owen says.

'They're all at it.'

Behind this conversation, I can hear David talking about his research.

'Half of it is luck,' David says. 'Your PhD is screwed if none of your experiments work out.' I hope Ruth and Mer aren't bored with him talking about science. Still, David works in cancer research, making him interesting to people he meets.

'Do you need a hand?' David calls out.

'No, no. Everything's under control.' I walk into the dining room with the crumble. 'Compliments of Mrs Murphy, my home economics teacher – this and scones are about as much as I can manage.' I serve the dessert, replenishing the wine glasses. David touches my back as I sit down.

I take a deep breath; now that the food is served I can relax and enjoy the evening. The coffees will be easy; actual cooking is like writing where lapses in concentration rarely go unpunished. Taking a mouthful of Merlot, my left hand rests on David's thigh and I'm distracted by thoughts of David's legs and ass, firm from cycling to and from Trinity. David smiles back. His hair has a quiff; I think it suits him better than his usual side-swept fringe, though I've never said it to him.

'So tell me about the new book? When is it coming out?' David asks Ruth.

'I still have another bit to go,' she replies, tucking her hair behind her ear. 'It might be rubbish.'

'It'll be brilliant,' I say. 'Look at the last one and the Orange Prize. Didn't I say you'd get the Booker?'

'Hardly,' Ruth laughs.

'Is this your second?' David asks.

'I'd tried other books before but that was the first one to get published.' I listen to Ruth's calm description of her work. Perhaps this was the difference between us; I'd always been eager and optimistic, perhaps even egotistical about my own work. Her steady discipline and stoic acceptance of the trials and failures of being a writer seem to have sustained her long after I gave up.

'I've been hoping to read some of his stories but he won't let me.' David nods his head in my direction, smiling at the others.

'I can't even look at them myself, they're so bad. I couldn't imagine going through that again.'

'Rubbish,' Mer says. 'Aren't you always writing because you're always thinking?'

She was quoting a famous female writer who'd spoken to us during our Master's. Larger than life, perfectly groomed and in her seventies, she measured every sentence as if each of her words was being transcribed. I've seen her interviewed on television since and heard her repeat the same lines but this is okay – maybe she says the same things because she's unravelled the secret of writing and life, and those few truths are the only things worth telling.

'What would you have been if you weren't a writer?' one of the graduates had asked her.

'I'd be in a madhouse,' was her entertaining yet immediate response.

'I'd say you'll go back writing,' Ruth says, taking a bite of crumble. 'Back to the addiction.'

I often joked about my desire to write, calling it pathological. I wrote five failed novels in my teens and early twenties, along with the short stories, after which my output slowed. At first, I thought it was like what'd happened to Philip Larkin; I wasn't losing steam but rather what I wrote was condensing into something of a superior quality. But the output continued to decrease as my life grew busier. It slowed to an odd hour's writing on a Saturday, and then nothing.

'What was the first thing you ever wrote?' James asks Ruth.

'I remember writing this story for a competition in school. It was awful.'

'I bet you won it though,' I laugh, almost certain that Ruth was a perfect student, whose sufferings were caused by her inability to get things wrong. It is strange that she has so much to write about when it appears she's made so few errors over the course of her life: married one man, raised a number of well-adjusted children, been happy.

The realisation of how well she's lived makes me inhale. How truthful would my fiction have to be if I decided to write again? Would I have to be 'private in public', as I've read all true artists had to be, confessing my secrets? Would that mean telling my friends – the world for that matter – how many people I've fucked? What was it anyhow – fifty, seventy… one hundred? And if I counted those I only 'fooled around with', the number probably doubled.

David has never asked me how many. I don't think it would break us up if I did tell him but it might tarnish things.

His perception would inevitably change and perception is everything; after all, the only difference between a plant and a weed is perspective.

Of course, there are funny stories that I could tell about my past, the anecdotes detailing my stupidity – getting ambulanced after drinking twelve raw eggs every day for a week in an attempt to bulk up, or the failed attempt at blending salad to save time (it turned into a prickly mush that tasted like nettles), or even that time I ate salmon twice a day, every day for six months in the vain attempt to avoid getting wrinkles (while concurrently spending my weekends binge drinking and doing coke).

'I couldn't do all that again,' I say finally, 'you know, sending off manuscripts, the waiting, the rejection. I don't know how you guys stick it out.'

Mer smiles.

'There's nothing else to do. It's the payment for doing what you love.'

Doing what they loved – it is the common thread that runs through the people in my life. Mer and Ruth love writing; David is passionate about his research; Owen and Mark ignore the rest of us as they debate the finer points of various Irish laws and statutes. Granted, I love my publishing job but there can be no forgetting the words I wrote in my personal statement when I applied for the Master's:

'The experience of writing, sitting down at a desk and beginning with an idea, only to look up and realise that a whole day has passed and I've been so engrossed that I've forgotten to eat. This is what I love…'

The stories are there again; the more I think about the past, the more anecdotes appear. I could write about that summer fucking the nineteen-year-old. I could describe the time I was blown by a drag queen. I might confess to all my old piercings, many years removed, or how I tried more than once to suck my own cock after I watched *Shortbus*. I might write how I measured my dick, wondering whether to calculate it by running a ruler up the outside from my balls, or from the inside, though it made me lose an inch. Some might find me freakish, but maybe, by confessing myself through fiction, I'd create a voice that would resonate with at least a few others.

I smile and lean sideways, my head resting on David's shoulder. I close my eyes for a moment, enjoying the darkness that allows the creative energy to rise higher. I feel David's warm lips on my forehead.

'You're wrecked,' David whispers.

'Not at all,' I reply; I lift my head and kiss him.

David collects the coats from the spare room. Mer and Ruth attempt to move the stained wine glasses and coffee cups from the table but I say that I'll clean them up afterwards. I decide that when they leave I'll get my laptop out and write for an hour. Lines and anecdotes seem plentiful, like the artefacts that fill my new home. The feeling of being a creator is there; I feel excited, even arrogant, that this might be the beginning of something unique, possibly a work of genius.

I know from experience how fleeting this urge to write is. Truth be told, by the time I've put the plates in the dishwasher and added the tablet and salts, the feeling may well have subsided and I may simply go to bed, get distracted by David, fuck and fall asleep.

But this is okay too. It is inevitable that the impulse to write will return before long because I, like everyone else, carry my ample past around with me.

THE GIFT

'This is the true joy in life, the being used for a purpose recognised by yourself as a mighty one... the being a force of nature instead of a feverish selfish little clod of ailments and grievances complaining that the world will not devote itself to making you happy.'

George Bernard Shaw, *Man and Superman*

'Look,' Ange whispers, pointing at the underwire of a bra that's lying underneath the pew in front of us. We laugh quietly. I imagine the possible scenarios that would lead to a bra wire getting lodged under a pew. Maybe it is as Ange says, that your one felt she'd enough support from God.

Ange is good for me in this respect; she makes me smile when I start taking things too seriously. It's my first time inside a church in a while; a year has passed since my father's funeral. I haven't been typically religious for quite some time; the word I'd use is spiritual, that vague term that people use when they're almost atheists but can't quite ignore the events that seem to be somehow intended. Like the day I decided to call my half-brother whom I hadn't spoken to in twenty years: as I searched for his contact details, the phone rang and there he was.

Maybe it's this superstition that makes me alternately stand and kneel in the church and throw a few coins into the collection plate when it comes round; it's just as likely to be the pressure I feel sitting next to my religious relatives, though. We're all here for my father's anniversary mass, but they are proper Catholics who know the lines of the rosary to say when the congregation answers the priest.

I whisper to my cousin, asking her about Father Winters, the priest who used to be here. I've always enjoyed his surname, like a character straight out of a Charles Dickens novel. But it never matched the person: instead of severe features and a sharp voice, he had an incredibly mild nature. An apologist for his own existence, 'I'm sorry but...' was the opening to nearly every remark he ever made.

My cousin warns me that the new priest 'goes on a little'; in fact, he's interminable. Distracted, I look around the church and am surprised to see that it is full, though it's mainly children and the elderly. I get a few glances; it happens a fair bit these days, since my paintings started selling in the US. There have been a good few articles in the national press, though I try not to pay any attention. End of the day, I paint because I like painting. I wouldn't bother with it otherwise.

I look up at the ceiling. I like its simplicity, freshly painted wood panels with lights hanging down from the arches, like planets just above my head. I've always wished I could like churches more, but I grow hesitant, reminded of newspaper headlines and scandals.

After mass, we walk up to the family grave and stand in silence for a few moments. Ange straightens a bunch of daffodils that has fallen over. She looks like she's about to say something but then she sees my expression and stays quiet. She stands close to me, wrapping her arm around my back, and I touch her belly. It's only six weeks. None of the rest of the family knows, not even Lorcan; we wouldn't want him telling the kids at school. It was all a bit of an accident. We were going through a rough patch for a while but we ended up drunk on New Year's and one thing led to another.

It's just as well, really. Ange was odd with me for a few months, and very distant when it came to sex. She'd let me do it all right but I could tell she was faking. When she took off her bra, she'd complain about her breasts, saying she didn't feel in the mood. There was a moment when I wondered if she was cheating, but I dismissed the idea straight away; she isn't the type. In fact, I've always thought the world is divided into two groups, cheaters and non-cheaters, and neither group can understand the other.

'Will we walk back to the car?' I ask Ange after a few minutes. I feel somewhat comforted by the grave, as strange as that sounds; I guess it's because it's next to the church where I was baptised as a child, where the seeds of something serious must have started within me all those years ago. I may have dismissed a God of white robes but I still believe in the magic that turns lights into orbs, half-worlds floating above us, or a surname into a novel; that things are not just normal, not even in a village in North Cork. And, in a way, wasn't the bra wire another sign of this, of the extraordinary in life and the humour in it? That's why I smiled as we made our way back to the car, even while dabbing my eyes with my gloves.

Ange has the coffee ready when I enter the kitchen. Since the news about the baby she's been making me breakfast again. Before Christmas she was busy with her writers' group and was even talking about getting a job. She volunteered over the summer at Lorcan's soccer camp, which seemed unusual, as neither of them liked the place. I wonder what would've happened without the news of the baby.

The radio is on. Ange smiles at me; she slips her hand inside my dressing gown and kisses me.

'I haven't brushed my teeth,' I say.

'Ah, give over,' she replies, lightly tugging my chest hair before walking back to the counter. I pick *The Guardian* and flick through the opening pages.

'Jesus,' I exclaim. 'Look at that, Ange.'

'Watch the language.' She glances at the door. But Lorcan is upstairs on his Playstation. I show her the picture. It's of an old man on a raft in the middle of the ocean. It's of an old man on a raft in the middle of the ocean, driftwood floating all around him; people's homes, I suppose. Underneath is the caption: 'Nine Miles out to Sea: Images from the Japanese Tsunami'.

The old man reminds me of my father; he has that same wiry build. There's a rescue boat inching towards him from the left-hand corner of the picture. The water is calm; the only ripples are from the advancing rescue boat. It looks almost peaceful. I think of my father and the memory of the church a month ago comes into my head. I begin to doubt what I felt that day; perhaps faith can only ever be temporary.

The image of the old man stays with me as I hop in the car and head to the gallery. I think about my childhood. Like most people, I learnt that bad things happened because it was God's will and all the rest of it. But studying evolution put an end to that fairy story.

My phone beeps as I pull away. I know it's Ange even before I open the message.

'Would you remember milk for later?'

The message annoys me. Sometimes I wonder how she can live on this plane of running errands and worrying about her love handles. I've tried talking to her before about the things that bother me – and maybe they are a bit airy-fairy – but she just looks at me like I'm half-mad.

An idea occurs to me that I might use the photo in a painting. Granted, I've got that huge commission to finish for New York in November – the bread and butter, so to speak. But then again, sometimes a painter just has to paint what he has to paint. I'd like to capture something about that rescue boat, a bit of hope in the midst of all that misery.

I frown as I pull the car up outside the gallery. (I can see Gráinne inside; she's wearing that black skirt again with the bit of a split at the back.) As nice as my idea for the painting is, it doesn't seem to carry much weight when placed against images of black sea flooding over the Japanese defences. Like the bra wire underneath the church pew, it's just more of my ridiculous middle-class Western sentimentalism. Still, human kindness is something to celebrate, to put faith in.

'How's the new painting coming on?' Gráinne asks, as she pops her head around from the main gallery. I've been working on my 'rescue' picture for a few months, a sort of guilty secret while I finish off the sea storm for New York. I haven't mentioned it to Ange but it's impossible to hide it from Gráinne. 'Do you want a coffee from the shop?'

'Sure,' I say. Gráinne is wearing a green silk blouse; I can see the outline of her black bra. I try not to look. It's been a bit awkward since we messed around last year. The baby meant I cooled it off, but once that line has been crossed it's very hard to keep things clean. It's mad, really: she's a sexy girl, only twenty-four, red-haired with pert tits and pale nipples, but I'd never leave Ange. It'd be nice if I could explain to Ange that I love her but that then there's this other part of me. I tried to talk to her once, that time she caught me out a few years ago, but she just didn't get it.

'Will you keep an eye on the desk?' Gráinne shouts out;

I hear the tap of her shoes move towards the door. Maybe I should let her go; I don't trust myself around her. But she's good at her job – she gets the commissions with her black bra and tight skirts, and who knows what sort of fireworks would kick off if I did let her go. Ange would find out and there'd be a whole fuckload of drama.

The door opens. I glance around. Gráinne is back with coffees and a copy of *The Guardian*.

'I thought you'd like a read,' she says. I smile. *The Guardian* – she knows me better than I know myself. She hovers, sipping on her coffee while I open the paper. 'It doesn't have star signs, does it?'

'Nah, not in *The Guardian*.' I'm relieved when the gallery door opens and Gráinne goes back out front. I hear her laughing with what sounds like an older man.

I glance through the first few pages, the usual stories about the recession and the euro failing. I've been lucky, really; the recession doesn't seem to have hit the rich across the water. The 'one per cent', as they're called. The commissions keep coming.

Then I see an article about a toddler hit by a car in China. The whole thing was caught on video camera and it's gone viral online. I finish the piece. Apparently the drivers left her for dead, as did six other passers-by; this idea makes me queasy. I glance at my MacBook and wonder if I should take a look at the video. I'm not sure I can, though I guess it's like so many things that I say I can't do; I don't want to be exposed to this sort of reality. But a vision of her comes into my head: the baby girl lies in the dirt, thrown flat by the car; then, still dazed, gets up and stumbles around, before getting hit by another. It'd almost be cartoonish if it were not for the fact that this is a real girl, not Sylvester the Cat or Wile

E. Coyote.

I sip my coffee, reminded of the time I once walked past an unconscious man on Merchants Quay in Cork City. I'd got the impression that he wasn't a 'typical alcoholic' but, like everyone else, I didn't bother to stop. I've often tried to convince myself that he was just a drunk or on drugs so I can absolve myself of the guilt of not helping.

I glance up. I can hear Gráinne's voice.

'There's a waiting list, of course but why don't you give me a buzz next week after I've had a word with Gearóid. I'm sure he'd be delighted…'

I pick up my paintbrush, hoping that when I next open a paper it'll be news that the little girl has survived. And yet, as I dip my brush in the cerulean blue, I wonder if I want the Chinese toddler to live because I have a vested interest in her future, or because I don't want to address the consequences of what it means to be unfeeling, the reality of what we may be. The thought unsettles me. I take a step back from the painting – a small raft at sea being rescued – and I realise that it's little more than sentimental bullshit.

'Are you sure the pink is all right? We don't even know it's a girl,' I say. The pink on the nursery walls is a brighter shade than I would like.

'It's a girl. I know it,' Ange replies. I continue painting the wall. The cot is draped in black bin liners, to protect it from the paint. I picked the cot up at an antiques auction and sanded it down. Ange thought it was too expensive but, as with most things in the house, she went along with me in the end. She strokes her stomach.

'I've packed my labour bag. The doctor said to have it ready.'

I stretch up with the roller, trying to be careful with the paint, but it catches on the raised tips of the Aertex, coating them pink. Swearing, I get a cloth and wipe the points. They remain off-white.

'We really should get that awful shite off the ceiling,' I say. In the background I can hear the sounds of Lorcan's television. One of the lads from his school is over for the weekend and they've only come out of the room to search for biscuits. I asked if they wanted a trip out on my boat but no luck. The Playstation has them hooked.

'It's a bit dark in here.' Ange flicks the switch but the light doesn't come on. She winces.

'Are you all right?'

'I'm fine. It's just a kick from her. You want a coffee? No, no, I'll get it. You've been working...' Her brow tenses. She takes a deep breath. 'Maybe I'd better sit.' Her face grows pale as she rests on the foot of the stepladder. She touches her stomach, bends forward for a moment, then stands up and hurries to the bathroom.

I hear her cry and push open the door. She stands, gazing at the blood in the toilet bowl, the crimson drops spreading, turning pink and translucent. I lift out my phone and dial for an ambulance. Lorcan calls out, 'are you all right, Mam?'

'We're fine, we're fine,' she shouts back. 'Just stay in your room.'

It's a warm September day and beads of sweat glisten on Lorcan's head as he and I carry the little coffin to the grave. It's white and heavier than I expected.

A couple of children from the village gaze over the grey wall into the churchyard. There's something dreamlike about the whole place, the thick, uncut grass, cluttered with mottled headstones.

Ange is quiet as she walks behind us with a few of the family. She carried our baby girl for a month even though she was dead; the doctor thought it'd help with the grieving. But I heard her crying in the shower.

The priest leads us along the moss-covered path to the far side of the graveyard where a small hole has been dug in the family plot. He says a few words as the coffin is lowered. I gaze at the engravings on the family headstone; the name of my father still looks fresh compared to the weathered lettering of the names above it.

Outside my four-hundred-dollar-a-night Times Square hotel bedroom I can hear the faint sound of sirens. It's eleven p.m. and I've just unveiled my commission to the Mayor and had dinner with a bunch of people from the New York art scene. I don't think the painting is my best work; in fact, I think it's shit. After what happened with the baby, I just got the thing done because I had to, not because I felt any desire to do so. I wanted to throw it in the skip along with that other painting.

I think of Ange going to the grave most days, even though the trip from Kinsale takes an hour. I was there when she brought the toys. Glass toys. She broke them so they wouldn't be stolen and laid them on the grave: a red octopus, a yellow cat, a green fish and a blue horse. They've grown dusty since then, covered in what looks like limescale. The wreaths are fading, reds mellowing into orange and yellow. One day there'll be nothing.

The kettle clicks off. I sigh and make myself a coffee. At least everyone else thought the painting was good. Gráinne is great with the PR – she made sure the heavyweights got behind it and then the rest followed. It's mad watching her network; I don't know what I'd do without her, really.

I glance at the jacket hanging off the wardrobe door, a two thousand euro Dolce and Gabbana tweed. On the floor beneath it is a pair of Gucci loafers. The money I got paid was ludicrous and I already have a number of commissions for when I go back to Kinsale. But right now I don't feel like doing any of them and I can't imagine that I will when I'm back either. I sip my coffee and stare out the window at the varying lights, and realise with a sense of irony that, after the early years of hardship, my life is now exactly as I always hoped it would be.

There is no trusting happiness. I think of Ange and our dead baby girl and know that my life is not the result of things working out because of some intangible fate. The New York success is due to luck or clever marketing; it will fall apart. It's like holding the brittle wing of an insect which, no matter how careful I am, will inevitably disintegrate. I have nothing left that's worth saying, nothing to paint about.

In a club, Gráinne slips me Adderall, a yellow diamond-shaped pill that she says her friend gave her. For a second I wonder am I too old to be taking it. Then I think 'fuck it', that I'm too old to be out clubbing in New York anyway, so I may as well go the whole hog. After twenty minutes, the drug feels like happiness, and maybe it is happiness, or as good as happiness can be. And I dance for hours and buy rounds and rounds of overpriced drink with my latest windfall.

Leaving the club at five a.m., the others go ahead while I walk through Chelsea with Gráinne; my feet are tired, though I find myself talking unnecessarily. Gráinne is rambling also, but I pay little attention, more preoccupied by the heat of my semi-hard cock against my thigh.

I've taken five a.m. walks like this before. I once wandered through the lanes of the Marais in Paris with another girl, the one Ange found out about. After dinner in the Hotel du Nord, the French receptionist and I kissed outside the toilets of a bar. She'd taken my jacket into the ladies' to rinse out a wine stain, and I hung by the door, waiting to catch her while she was alone.

On her bedside locker there were a number of books.

'I'm glad you read,' I said. The coke we'd taken earlier was making me waffle. 'Who was it said that if someone doesn't read you shouldn't have sex with them?'

'Who says we're going to have the sex?' she smiled back at me.

Her skin was smooth to the touch. Sitting up, she opened the locker and took out a packet of condoms.

'Anything interesting in there?' I glanced at the drawer but her hand reached downwards. Her fingers were cold

'Fuck,' I inhaled. She smiled.

I remember the French girl as I glance at Gráinne. I try not to think about Ange. Instead I think about kissing Gráinne, licking her nipples, but then I feel anxious about how she'll react if I make my excuses and leave.

We walk underneath the High Line Park and I catch a glimpse of the dried grasses hanging over the sides of the old metro line barriers and, for a moment, I wish I was home in Ireland.

Gráinne looks at me, smiling; she must think I've stopped so we can avail of the High Line's shadow. I wonder would it be easier to do the polite thing, fuck her and forget about it. After all, we've done it before and is it really any different now?

However, as she leans in I stop her, glancing at my watch and mentioning my early start. I smile, hoping if I appear awkward she'll accept the rejection nicely. She's gracious if a little cajoling. I assume she's trying to play it cool, and I wonder if Gráinne is really the girl I think she is; that perhaps she's another nice girl whom, in some other life, I might've dated and fallen in love with, though most likely I'd have fucked her over, just like I have poor Ange.

I feel relieved when we finally say goodnight in the lobby and I walk back to my room, take some sleeping pills, brush my teeth and slip into the large cool bed.

I arrive at MoMA a little after lunchtime; the Adderall has worn off and my enthusiasm for art feels diminished after four days of sightseeing, schmoozing and late-night dinners with art critics. I know I did the right thing by going to my hotel room alone and yet I feel resentful. Behaving well does not make me feel good; it feels like I've missed out on something.

The queue for tickets is long. I look at the counters, trying to catch the attention of a good-looking girl at the third desk, my resentment rising higher. I'm hoping she might recognise who I am if we do catch each other's eye. But when it comes my turn to pay I'm directed towards a middle-aged lady. It's probably just as well.

I make my way to the top floor of MoMA to see the De Kooning exhibit, which I find uninteresting and devoid of talent; just another artist taking the piss. Not that I blame De Kooning; am I not doing the same, painting lies, making a few quid by convincing the gullible of my genius?

I pause as a tour group passes and listen to their guide, knowing how easy it is to say anything about anything. I wrote essays for my degree in the Crawford, thousands of words long, about white canvases and half-assed sketches that were not worth the frames they were mounted in. Those essays were just more bullshit to add to the mounting piles of it in the world, all trying to make out there's something more when there isn't.

Sick of De Kooning, I glide down the escalators to the floor below and enter a gallery of postmodern art, only to be reminded of a South Park episode called 'Growing up is Hard to Do', where everything in Stan's life is transformed into literal shit as he sees the world for what it is. I look at the pointless installations, ridiculous leaning piles of pipes in the corners of white spaces and bricks stacked in the centre of rooms, and wonder if there is anything in the gallery that couldn't be found in a typical skip.

I glance at my watch, thinking it's likely I'll be in and out of MoMA within the hour (at a cost of eighteen dollars). Looking at the map, I walk into the Impressionists room, reasoning that once I've seen the Monets I'll be free to leave without having to feel guilty. After all, if someone asks if I've been to MoMA, I'll be able to say, 'yes, the Monets were superb'; a banal answer to match the banal experience of viewing them. Truth be told, I think Impressionist paintings are too pretty, just bright splashes of colour; a glossy, deluded reality.

I enter the gallery and Monet's *Water Lilies* is impossible to miss; the canvas is forty feet by ten feet at least. I'm surprised by the rising heartbeat in my chest. My eyes start to tingle. Maybe it's the Adderall comedown, or the alcohol, or the lack of sleep, but something within me alters. My mood lifts, something which would've seemed impossible just moments before. I feel the hairs on my arms stand up, a response that feels almost religious (as crazy as that sounds).

As I move into the centre of the room, the painting takes over the whole of my view. I begin to realise that it is not the result of random splashes of paint, rather the considered work of a genius.

Moving closer, I examine the paint applied with only the illusion of spontaneity, colours incorporated layer after layer, creating numerous paintings in one. I can see not only lilies but also swathes of pattern that suggest not simply water but galaxies, the whole cosmos stretched out before me. Yet even without these impressions of infinity, the colours themselves are enough to make my eyes water, though I can't quite figure out why.

I cry. I've caught a glimpse of a reality so vast that I wonder if it is actually the true life and the world around it nothing more than a mediocre frame. The endless layers of thick paint and the swathes of colour and light reflect a more powerful world than any I've existed in.

I stand still for many minutes, wanting to understand the extra sense that Monet possessed that, even at late in life, allowed him to see without apathy. Was it as the writer once said, that the artist is an 'individual endowed with a particular sort of sense which the human race of his generation does not possess'?

And yet I wonder was it that Monet had an extra sense or that he was missing one. Had his actual blindness allowed him to see a more real world, like the deaf Beethoven who heard true beauty when he wrote the Ninth Symphony?

I leave the room of lilies and walk back into the postmodern galleries. It's as though Monet's *Water Lilies* was the key and now I can see clearly for the first time. Here is the reality I'd lost. These artists whose work I am surrounded by are attempting to make me see my own world with renewed vigour, to see it in novel ways, to transform the ordinary. They make the familiar strange and vice versa, so I can look at things not just as acquired objects but as metaphor; think about the world, about me, in ways beyond the literal.

The perfect rectangle of foil-wrapped sweets sitting on the gallery floor is no longer simply confectionery; Félix González-Torres has revealed it as a path to transcendence. Carl Andre's brick sculptures aren't a 'fuck you' to the viewer – an 'I can put a neat stack of bricks in a gallery and call it art' – but an act of love, so that I might see something as mundane as construction material as if it were water that I might wade in, a whole geometric world that I might dive into if I allowed myself to embrace this new perception. In seeing these works, I am not seeing just a new world but also a new self.

In art, in front of Monet's *Water Lilies*, I rediscover my path. Using my brush, I can transfigure the literal world, continue seeing it anew. What is the past but a canvas on which to paint my own truths, be my own benevolent God? And is it not the same with the future? The present, in many ways, I cannot change materially. I cannot prevent children dying or stop tsunamis killing whole populations. Nor can I undo my past mistakes or bring my baby girl back to life. But I can show others a new way of seeing, another way for life to be; and maybe this perception, if believed by enough people, might change the literal world. My lie might become truth.

I smile, thinking about the new eyes I've just acquired. For, without these eyes, if I saw a bra wire underneath a pew as part of an installation in MoMA, I would scoff, thinking it was simply a device by an artist to get noticed for being sacrilegious. I wouldn't consider it art at all, let alone something that might exist in the literal world.

And yet there was a bra wire under a pew in a church in North Cork.

Surely that meant something.

Acknowledgements

A big thank you my sister Beverly and her husband Gavin: without their patience and generosity, I'm certain this book would not have been possible. Orlene Denice McMahon deserves a special mention for her love and unwavering belief in my writing. My gratitude to Claire, Susan, Colin, Ronan and Noel, whose views, reviews and criticism have helped me to refine the collection into what it is today. I'm indebted to the staff of Cork City Library for their endless support over the past decade, to my professors in University College Dublin whose advice during my Master's has proved invaluable, and to Ann Luttrell of the Triskel for having faith in a fledgling writer.

My thanks to editor extraordinaire Aoileann Lyons for making me coherent, Fidelma Maye for all her encouragement and sound advice, and all the team at Tigh Filí Cultural Centre. Finally, a huge thank you to Máire Bradshaw for publishing my book and helping me to realise a dream that I've been chasing for as long as I can remember.

About the Author

JAMIE O'CONNELL was born in Ireland in 1984. He was the 2011 Writer in Residence for Tigh Filí Cultural Centre and toured the United States with the Cork Literary Review Volume XIV Editor Eugene O'Connell, presenting work in San Francisco, Chicago, Boston and New York. He has an MA in Creative Writing from University College Dublin and a BA in English Literature from University College Cork. He lives in Cork City.

For more information visit www.jamieoconnellwriter.com.